The chronicles of Godfrey
an allegory

The secret history of Manchester and the whole world actually.

Don Egan

Copyright © Don Egan 2013

The right of Don Egan to be identified as author of this work has been asserted by him in accordance with the Copyright, Designs and Patents Act 1988.

All rights reserved.

ISBN-13: 978-1494301712
ISBN-10: 1494301717

By the same author

Searching for Home - a journey of the soul.

Beautiful on the Mountains - autobiography.

Healing is coming!

Dedicated to
the lovely people of
Manchester
and the North West.

Contents

PART ONE

The Olden Times	11
Godfrey has an idea	13
Godfrey finds the stopcock	23
The place of Man	29
Opposition	37
Albert and Edna	41
The White Rat	49
Norman builds a boat	59
The Tower of Blackpool	69
Blood and stars	75
The surrogate affair	79
The Barbecue	85
The Brickworks	97
The Lighthouse	109
Red Lights and Red Rope	115
Brass band	127
Big Gordon	131
The Bad Sheila Affair	139
Old Sam goes to town	151
A most expensive pearl	159
The wise and foolish builder	169
The swarm of locusts	177
The Prophet Malarkey	181

PART TWO

The Newer Times	185
The road from Wigan	187
Eric goes on a mission	195
While shepherds washed their socks by night	203
The child killer	209
Godfrey invents the serum	215
The trainees	225
Jack gets angry	235
Breaking bread	241
The incident at Southern Cemetery	253
The Lamb of Godfrey	259
Hurricane Sophia	267
Afterwards	273
About the author	275
Connect	275

Warning

You are about to enter a new world. While parts of this new world look and sound like the world we humans live in, other parts seem very different, improbable and at times unbelievable. It is a world not unlike the dream world that we encounter when we sleep – simple things that should happen become difficult, while complicated things that are impossible happen freely as a matter of course.

But this world actually exists. This world goes on every day, inside my head, and I blame my Dad.

When I was four-years-old, I was walking down the street with my Dad. I looked at the traffic lights and asked him how they worked. He told me that there was a little pixie inside the traffic lights whose job was to run up and down a ladder, lighting and blowing out three candles, and that's how traffic lights worked.

For a brief moment I looked at the traffic lights, and I imagined the little pixie running up and down his little ladder. A moment later I knew my Dad was teasing me. But it was too late. Since that day, inside my head, there has always been an alternative explanation for everything.

Unless you come to this new world as a little child,

you won't be able to enter.

To be fair to my Dad, how else would you explain something as complex as the workings of traffic lights to a little child? You could boggle their mind with a complicated explanation they wouldn't be able to grasp. Or you could tell them a story.

When we ask the deep questions, I am not sure a complicated and technical answer is always helpful. But if you can tell me a story that makes me think, I can come to my own conclusions. The older I get, the more I prefer stories.

In all the different cultures around the world, stories are used to explain why things are the way they are.

The world you are about to enter is different from any other world or culture you have ever visited. Sometimes you'll think you have a grasp on it and then it will surprise you.

This story is the result of a question I asked myself: 'What would the world be like if God lived near Oldham?'

As I tried to answer that question, I soon found myself in this new world where anything can happen and often does. This world has its own rules and laws of nature. That is why you need to come as a little child.

I grew up in Manchester, and the wonderful people and places of that great city, and the surrounding areas, shaped me in my early years of life. Now, for the first time, I can reveal to the people of Manchester how their world was formed, and why it is like it is. This is the secret history of Manchester. In fact, this is the secret history of the whole world.

PART 1

The Olden Times

1

Godfrey has an idea

Long ago, on the far side of yesterday, in the times when the River Irwell was only a tiny trickle of angel tears that meandered through a barren land, there was an old tower on the hill at Hartshead Pike, near the Mountains of Ninepence. A very old hermit named Godfrey, who wore green dungarees, lived in the tower. Godfrey had thick black hair, a rather large nose, and magical powers.

Godfrey liked the outdoor life and, when he was not reading books or eating porridge in his tower, he would walk for miles on the Mountains of Ninepence. In the summertime, Godfrey would hard-boil some eggs and magic up a packet of crisps and a bottle of dandelion and burdock, and walk all the way to Glossop. (I say Glossop but I mean where Glossop is today – in those days the area had no houses or any such thing, because people hadn't been invented yet.) There he would sit by the river eating his eggs and crisps, and drinking his dandelion and burdock. Sometimes, on the walk back to his tower at Hartshead Pike, he would do a really loud burp that tasted of dandelion and burdock. That always made him laugh, though he was not sure why.

One Sunday morning, Godfrey sat on the doorstep of his tower, having a brew and some toast in the sunshine, when he had an idea. He thought it was the best idea he'd ever had. Instead of just creating crisps and dandelion and burdock with his magic powers, what if he created some creatures who were quite like him? What would that be like? He began making drawings and plans, and writing down his ideas. He always had to be careful when he made changes to the world, so he thought deeply about his idea. Godfrey had been feeling a bit down for quite a while but this new idea seemed to lift his spirits. He began calculating all the pros and cons, and the whys and whatnots. Some nights he worked until the sun came up on tomorrow, and the candle in the old wine bottle had burned down to the top of the bottle and dropped inside it.

One sunny morning he stood at his front door in his slippers and his green dressing gown, drinking his brew and pondering his new idea. 'What we need,' he said to himself, 'is to start small.' All the best things start small, he thought. Maybe he'd just create one person, and put them in a beautiful garden. But where should the garden be?

As he watched the breeze blowing across the grassy slopes, he remembered a dry, bleak area he had to cross on his way to Glossop in the summer. It stretched all the way from the Mountains of Ninepence as far West as Warrington. (I say Warrington but I mean where Warrington is today. In those days... well, you get the picture.)

'That area will be the place where I shall create the garden and the new creature. I will call him 'man',' he decided. But how would he bring life to such a dry, barren place he wondered?

Creating such creatures was far more complicated than trying to magic up dandelion and burdock or crisps. This magic would require some additional wisdom and a touch of the ancient knowledge. Godfrey pondered, and then pondered a bit more. Magic hermits do a lot of pondering before they create something.

That evening, in the cool of the day, he sat down on the doorstep of his tower, smoking his pipe, when a blackbird flew over his head and through the open door into the tower. Godfrey dropped his pipe, scattering ashes across the doorstep. The bird began to panic because it could not find its way out of the tower. Godfrey jumped up and grabbed an old fishing net, which was leaning against the hat stand. The bird saw the high windows in the tower and flew upwards, looking for an escape. Godfrey ran up the staircase to the first floor balcony, which was lined with old books all the way round the tower. The bird squawked and flapped and Godfrey waved the net around in the air like a hermit possessed. The bird, exhausted from the commotion, landed on the top shelf of the bookcase panting for breath. Godfrey lurched at the bird with the net and yanked it towards him, bringing half a dozen books, off the top shelf, tumbling down to the floor. He cupped the bird firmly in his hands and walked downstairs to the door, where he released the bird to freedom. The blackbird, slightly dazed by the experience, flew off towards where Oldham is today.

Godfrey went indoors and started to tidy up the mess. He went upstairs to the balcony and began collecting up the books strewn across the floor. As he did, he grunted as he lifted the biggest one. It was very heavy and covered in dust. It had not been off the shelf in ages. Godfrey looked at the cover – *"EARTH: Owner's Repair & Maintenance Manual – by Godfrey Oliver Davis"*. Godfrey put the other books down, sat on the top step, and flicked through the pages of the ancient tome. He remembered some of the information although he had not consulted the book for many centuries. Everything had run well for ages, apart from a serious altercation with a particularly unpleasant boggart at Blackley.

Boggart

A boggart is a malevolent creature inhabiting fields, marshes or holes in the ground. Boggarts love to steal, kill and destroy. They turn milk sour, cause accidents and love darkness.

Wondering if the book had any suggestions as to how he could begin to irrigate the proposed place of man, Godfrey turned to section 3874 - "Plumbing, rainfall, and adjusting local climates." There he found the information he needed.

'Local climates, and in particular rainfall, may be adjusted by the nearest stopcock. These are situated

at various locations around the earth. They are usually sited in extremely secret places in order to remain hidden from troublesome boggarts, who delight in causing droughts and floods by meddling with the Earth's control system. For your nearest stopcock please see Appendix 65,792.'

Godfrey located Appendix 65,792, which told him that the nearest stopcock to the proposed place of man was in the deep valley of Woodhead, a good day's walk away from his tower.

Next morning after some porridge, a brew and a smoke of his pipe, Godfrey set off towards the valley of Woodhead. In his backpack were four Glossop eggs, three packets of crisps, and three bottles of dandelion and burdock. By mid morning he had reached a small wooded area called Mossley. He took off his backpack and sat on the ground. He leaned against a tree in the shade at the edge of the woods. He listened to the birds singing. His head was still full of ideas about the place of man he was going to create. He ate two boiled eggs and a packet of crisps, washed down by a bottle of dandelion and burdock.

He was so happy on this day. His thoughts were all about this new creature he would be able to chat to and share the joys of life with on the beautiful earth. Satisfied by his walk and his lunch, Godfrey closed his eyes. In the distance he could hear a cuckoo. He smiled. The world was good. It was really, really good. Deep in the woods, he could hear a Green Woodpecker laughing. His smile broadened. He had given the Green Woodpecker a heightened appreciation of humour precisely so that it would laugh more often than other birds. He drifted into an unexpected nap with a smile on his face. All the late nights of planning and pondering had caught up with him.

Godfrey awoke with a start. A black cloud covered the sky. He felt cold. A deep foreboding overshadowed his heart. He had visited a dark place – a nightmare. He felt anxious, which was very unusual for a magic hermit in those days. He began to think about the altercation with the boggart at Blackley, and kept turning it over in his mind. Whichever way he thought about that incident, he couldn't have done things any differently, and certainly could not have done better. Boggarts were boggarts – independent, selfish, destructive and arrogant. Those were the facts. You had to take them into account but you couldn't let them control your plans. Quite what the nightmare had been, Godfrey couldn't really remember, but he was more determined to press on with creating the place of man. He loved new beginnings.

He stood up, pulled a green cloak out of his backpack and wrapped it around himself. He slung the backpack over his shoulder and set his face towards the Valley of Woodhead. The ground was muddy, spongy and made of peat in this area. He trudged on, his legs becoming heavy. He came over the top of a small mound at Swineshaw and paused for a moment. A pig lifted its snout from the mud and stared at him. He looked beyond the pig to see many more pigs foraging in the mud and the peat. He had created pigs a while back and thought they would be his new companions. But they only seemed interested in poking their snout into the ground searching for food. It was not exactly a failed experiment - they were interesting creatures as were all the others he had made. It was just that pigs were not great company when you were having a brew, smoking a pipe, or telling stories over a glass of wine in the evening. And no matter how many times you washed them and cleaned them up, they always returned to the dirt. They didn't even laugh like the Green Woodpecker either. Mostly they grunted and squealed.

As Godfrey crossed this muddy plateau, all the pigs looked at him knowingly. They knew who he was. Many heads paused, glanced and bowed in his direction. Without Godfrey, they would not exist. And every one of them was as happy as a pig... well, as happy as a pig in mud. He had made them to be happy in mud. And they were.

Godfrey reached the far side of Swineshaw and began to wonder about where he would spend the night. He came to the foothills of the Mountains of Ninepence and followed the contour of the land South. Eventually he knew he would find the entrance to the Valley of Woodhead, though the day was far spent, and finding the stopcock would have to wait until morning.

As darkness began to descend over the land, Godfrey reached Anak's Castle – the only building in Tintwistle. Anak was the king of the Giants, who walked the earth in those days. Anak was indeed a king but there were only seventeen giants living, in the whole of the earth, so the title was more a thing of history than of power. Anak's real power was that he was fifteen feet tall and would eat a whole cow just for a snack. But he was a kindly giant, if you weren't a cow that is, and on the rare occasions Godfrey went to visit his castle, Anak loved Godfrey's stories, and eating, and drinking, and laughing with him well into the night. Anak's burps were more disturbing than Godfrey's as the whole castle would shake, and the smell of a giant's burp could make you gag.

As it turned out, Anak arrived at his castle shortly after Godfrey. The giant was carrying a bundle of trees under one arm and a sack of meat over the opposite shoulder. Anak's face beamed when he saw Godfrey.

'Well, well! Look who has come to visit the lonely giant today. Godfrey, my dear friend, how wonderful to see you. Go in. Go in.' The pair chatted as Anak lit a fire. He began to cook the various joints of meat and make a brew.

After Anak had locked the door for the night, he and Godfrey sat by a roaring fire in the main hall, eating roast beef, steaks, and other sections of cow. Anak drank wine by the bucket, but he always kept a small hermit-sized glass for when Godfrey came to visit.

Whenever the flames died down, Anak would reach forward and lift another tree onto the fire.

Godfrey put his wine glass down and pulled out his pipe. He loaded it and pointed his finger at it. A flame shot from his finger and lit the pipe. They both laughed at the fun of magic powers. Anak's laugh made the castle shake.

Godfrey looked into the flames and was quiet for a moment.

'Anak, I may need your help tomorrow.'

For the first time, Godfrey began to share his plan for creating the place of man. Anak sensed the seriousness of the moment and listened closely.

After Godfrey finished, Anak looked at him intently. The fire crackled. The shadows of the two friends danced on the castle walls.

'Godfrey, my dear friend,' Anak said, 'if there is anything I can do to help you, you know I will. I may be big on the outside, but you are the true giant – you are a giant on the inside. And that, my friend, is far more powerful. As always, my friend, the King of the Giants bows to the true King of kings on Earth.'

Nothing more was said that night. Both of them watched the fire. When it became a few glowing embers, Anak looked up, intending to show Godfrey to his room. But Godfrey was gone. He knew his room was always kept ready there, and he had silently withdrawn while Anak was still fire-gazing.

Anak didn't go to bed that night. He stared into the embers of the fire for hours. He began to feel the weight of his friend's burden. He felt honoured to have Godfrey as a friend, let alone a guest. This night had been different. They had certainly laughed that night, but not as much as on previous visits. Godfrey was carrying something. It was a good thing. But it seemed to weigh heavy on him. As Anak drifted to sleep he wondered how he could help his friend.

2

Godfrey finds the stopcock

Anak woke with a stiff neck, having slept the night in his giant chair by the fire. It was early and the sound that woke him from his slumber was beautiful. It was a sound he didn't hear often enough. It was, at the same time, gentle and like the sound of many waters. As he stood up, the sound was now like a trumpet calling to the distance. Then like the deep sound of a cello, and then like running water. He knew what the sound was and it filled him with joy. Godfrey was standing on the castle roof, singing a song to the world he had created. The song told every living thing in the kingdom how beautiful it was. And Godfrey rejoiced over every creature with singing.

This beautiful sound had another effect, in the Earth. It caused every boggart who heard the sound to flee into their holes in the ground, and ram their fingers in their ears. They could not stand the sound at all.

On this day, Godfrey was also calling to Sophia. Whenever Godfrey sang this song, it was never long before Sophia appeared. There really was no other way of contacting her apart from a holy silence. She came and went as she chose. Often unseen and yet you felt her presence like the wind. Other times she was present and you wouldn't even be aware of her.

Anak lit a fire and put the kettle on for a brew. Soon Godfrey came downstairs from the roof and joined Anak, who now had eggs and bacon cooking over the fire. The pair ate their breakfast in silence. Godfrey was pondering again and Anak didn't want to interrupt his friend's thoughts. Unfortunately, he failed to hold in a mighty giant burp after breakfast, and the sound and the smell brought Godfrey out of his contemplations.

'Thanks for sharing that, Anak! Let us get on our way.'

The pair of friends set off from Anak's Castle and entered the valley heading towards Crowden. As they walked along, Anak became aware of a strange creature that seemed to be tracking them from the top of the hillside.

'Ignore him,' whispered Godfrey.

'I think it's a boggart,' said Anak.

'It is a boggart,' said Godfrey. 'No doubt sent here to spy for Owd Hob. Just ignore him. I've already made plans to deal with him.'

Anak followed close behind Godfrey but kept one eye on the ugly creature scurrying on the top of the hill. Godfrey did not really need protecting – he was Godfrey. But Anak was used to protecting his friends due to his size. He had friends even though this was before the days of man. Back in those days several strange creatures that have now died away still existed. Some of them had even written books. But like the giants, their numbers were dwindling to dangerously small numbers. He could not help feeling he was Godfrey's bodyguard on this mission, even though the idea was ridiculous.

When the friends reached the Valley of Crowden, Godfrey paused and took out a bottle of dandelion and burdock and had a couple of swigs. Anak was staring at the boggart who was trying to hide on the hillside.

Godfrey took his notebook from his backpack and flicked to the page where he'd taken down some notes from the Earth Owner's Manual.

'We are very close now,' said Godfrey. 'But the boggart mustn't know that.'

'Shall I chase him away for you?' asked Anak.

'No. They are tricky characters – they have a network of holes and tunnels all over the Earth. He'll just hide from you and pop up somewhere else. Let us just be quiet for a moment.'

The two friends sat quietly in the sunshine. The boggart stared intently at them from behind a tree.

Godfrey began to sing the song of creation again but more quietly this time. The boggart cringed and screwed up his face. He hated that sound. It went right through him.

Godfrey stopped singing and waited. The boggart opened his eyes again, though he felt very uncomfortable he wanted to know what Godfrey was up to in these hills.

Anak felt a sudden breeze on his face. The wind seemed to be coming from all four directions at once. Then in the distance he saw a dazzling figure. He squinted to make out the details but the light coming from it was just too bright. Blinking and squinting to protect his eyes, he thought he saw a person. A person not just made of light but the most beautiful female he had ever seen.

The boggart squealed in pain as the lady made of light approached the pair of friends. He couldn't bear the sight or the sound and fled from the scene.

'It's Sophia,' whispered Godfrey, smiling at the figure approaching them. Anak had heard stories of Sophia but this was the first time he had ever seen her. Though he couldn't really see her – she was just too bright to look at. Godfrey tapped Anak on the shin – that was as high as he could reach – and motioned for the giant to walk with him. Neither of them looked back but, by the long shadows stretching in front of them, they knew Sophia was following. They arrived at Woodhead, where the valley ended. In front of them the ground rose steeply up onto the Mountains of Ninepence. Godfrey located the exact end of the valley and found the huge boulder he was looking for.

'Anak, can you lift this boulder for me?'

Even with the mighty strength he possessed, the giant struggled to lift the boulder. But eventually he did, rolling it onto its side. Godfrey stepped forward into the indentation in the ground where the boulder had been. Sophia stayed silent but sat on top of the boulder to shed her light into the hole, so Godfrey could see what he was doing. As she sat on the great rock, what had been a dark grey stone seemed to come to life. Moss and tiny flowers seemed suddenly to grow on the rock wherever Sophia touched it.

Godfrey used a piece of flint to scratch at the ground. Eventually he found it – a small triangular stone. He lifted one corner to reveal a rusty old stopcock. He tried to turn it on but it was stuck.

'Hmmm. By my calculations we need to get this thing to turn about half way round, but I can't get it to move.'

He motioned to Anak to help turn the ancient tap. Anak knelt down to the ground. Even he was struggling to turn the thing. Eventually there was a snapping and Anak fell forward. The tap was on. Unfortunately, he had snapped the top of the tap off. It was now on at three quarters; a bit more than Godfrey had calculated to bring life to the place of Man.

'Sorry!' said Anak.

'No worries,' said Godfrey. 'This place of Man will just be a bit wetter and have more rain than I was planning.'

Water began seeping from the valley floor. The three friends climbed up the side of the valley to Crowden. There they sat and watched as the Woodhead Valley filled with water and became a great lake.

The water continued to flow so that the whole of the long valley they had walked from Tintwistle became several great lakes. When the water level settled, Sophia walked towards it and, as Godfrey and Anak watched, as much as they could, dazzled by her piercing light, they saw her walk out onto the surface of the water. Every time she took a step, fish appeared beneath her feet. And every footstep produced a mist that rose up and formed clouds that drifted towards the place of Man.

Now a river flowed out of the lakes at Woodhead to water all the land of the place of Man, and from there it parted and became four river heads. Sophia walked down the lakes and then along a river towards the place of Man. As she did, life sprang up all around. Plants and shrubs burst into life. Rain fell from the sky. Sophia walked like this, creating life, all the way to the Irwell River. As the sun began to set, she found a spot she particularly liked and rested there for the night.

Godfrey caught a lift on Anak's shoulders back to the castle. He collected his things, said farewell to Anak, and set off for home. It was already dark by the time he reached Hartshead Pike. The tower was silhouetted against a moonlit sky. Godfrey went in and found a candle. He lit it, and pushed it into the old wine bottle on his desk. He set a small fire in his fireplace, pulled the cork on a bottle of wine, and sat slouched in the chair, staring at the fire. He sipped the wine and smiled. Today had been a great day, he thought to himself. Together they had provided living water for the place of Man. No longer was it dry and barren. If anything, it was going to be a tad wetter than most other places on the Earth. Godfrey chuckled at the thought and rested his eyes for a moment and, before anyone could say 'bash-a-boggart', he was snoring in the chair.

3

The place of Man

Next morning, Godfrey sat on the front step of his tower, enjoying the first brew of the day. There was always something special about the first brew of the day. As he surveyed the view he saw something moving in the sky. It was coming towards him, too big for a bird. It was a figure that seemed to be waving at him. Godfrey smiled as he recognised the approaching visitor.

The glowing white figure dropped gently from the sky and landed in front of the tower.

'Turned out nice again!' said the visitor smiling.

'Michael. How wonderful to see you,' said Godfrey. 'Brew?'

'Ooh ta! I'm knackered after that journey,' said Michael, folding his wings behind him.

The friends hugged and laughed. They went into the back kitchen and put the kettle on.

'Ay up! I brought you some angel cake,' said Michael, presenting the cake to Godfrey and chuckling to himself.

Godfrey smiled and rolled his eyes. 'You angels and your cake.'

Michael stirred the pot and found a plate for the cake. 'I've just come up from the place of Man. Sophia has been busy and made a wonderful place. She is resting now, near the willow tree.'

'The willow tree?' asked Godfrey.

'Oh yes, there is such life down there now. Where the River Irwell meets the River Irk, there is a great willow tree. It was the first thing Sophia planted. It is full of life, and all around it life springs up. The Irwell and the Irk, once only tiny trickles on a barren landscape, are now mighty rivers, flowing with clear crystal waters and teeming with life.' Michael could hardly contain himself as he bit into the slice of angel cake he had been waving about during his description.

'Wonderful,' said Godfrey, looking to the horizon. 'Wonderful.'

'Cake, Godfrey! Have some cake! You'll need cake for the day you are about to have!' Michael laughed.

'Oh by the way, on the way here I called in on Jack, at Brookdale. He asked if we could go by his place. He wants to join us on the way.'

'Ah, my lovely Jack. I miss him being at home. But your kids need to fly the nest sometime.'

'Well I can certainly fly from any nest,' said Michael. 'But I don't know anything about having kids, obviously, being an angel an' all that! More cake?'

'Now Michael, I need to ask you if you have arranged for your people to be with us tomorrow. We need maximum security.'

'Ah yes. Every angel on the planet will be there!'

said Michael. 'You know how they stood open-mouthed when you made the sky. And that day you made the sea at Blackpool and then the trees and stuff. They can't stop talking about some of the wonderful creatures you made. And ever since some of our number attempted to overthrow you, they are more determined than ever to protect the wonders you make. We lost a third of my army in the rebellion, but rest assured Godfrey, those who remain are loyal to you, Jack, and Sophia. We have been humbled by your constant kindness to us. We can't imagine what tomorrow will bring. Ever since our Gabriel briefed the rest of us yesterday, we have been so excited!'

'Michael, I'm well pleased. It seems we are prepared. If I know boggarts, they will have got wind of something going on, and they will try to disrupt it. Any road, help me wash up the cups and plates and then we can be off.'

Godfrey stood at the sink in the back kitchen of the tower. He always washed and Michael always dried. Godfrey liked to wash because he liked things clean. He wasn't obsessed but he did tend to wash and clean quite a bit. It was just how he was.

'Righto Chuck!' said Michael, putting the last cup he'd dried in the cupboard. 'Shall I fly you to the place of Man then?'

'Erm no,' said Godfrey, staring out of the kitchen window. 'I want to go slowly. You angels travel far too fast. How you don't have accidents I'll never know! We'll go on my tandem.' It was a lovely warm summer day. Hope and expectation filled the air as the two friends set off on the tandem towards the place of Man. As Godfrey steered the bike down the lane, the lilies on either side of the track bowed as he passed. The route to the place of Man was hilly, and they rolled down one hill and then got off and pushed the tandem up the next. After they pushed the bike up from Daisy Nook to Crime Lake, they sat down for a few moments' rest. They looked across the hills and could still see Godfrey's tower at Hartshead Pike.

'Ee, it's quite a ride is that. Cake?' said Michael, offering Godfrey more angel cake.

'Don't mind if I do,' said Godfrey, offering Michael a swig of dandelion and burdock.

The pair walked round the edge of the lake for a bit and began skimming little flat stones across the surface of the water, seeing who could make their stone skip the most number of times before it sank.

'Righto!' said Michael, after a few minutes. 'We better get a wriggle on.'

The pair got back on the bike and set off for Brookdale to meet up with Jack. As they rolled downhill on the track that ran near the River Medlock, the changes became more evident. The Medlock was no longer a tiny trickle but beautiful crystal clear river with flourishing plants and trees on both banks.

'It's lemonade!' shouted Michael, from the back seat of the tandem.

'What?' said Godfrey, thinking he hadn't heard properly.

'Lemonade! Sophia made the Medlock flow with Lemonade! When you walk by it you can scoop a handful of the finest lemonade and have a slurp. Lovely!'

Godfrey smiled.

The pair came to the bottom of Rosehey Lane and pushed the bike up the hill towards the woods that bordered Jack's estate at Brookdale. They found the narrow gate and cycled up the long drive. Perfect lawns with formal flowerbeds bordered the driveway. Peacocks stood on the lawns and squawked to welcome them and announce their arrival to Jack.

Jack lived in a big white mansion in the centre of the estate. The house was square with four bedroom windows on the upper floor. It had four chimney-stacks, one at each corner. On one side of the house was a glass summerhouse and at the front was a large portico with four pillars at the entrance.

'Anyone home?' called Godfrey as they reached the front door.

'Round the back!' came a voice from round the corner.

There they found Jack building a new chair.

'Ay up, our Dad! How are you?'

'Put the kettle on, Lad,' said Godfrey.

'Anyone for cake?' said Michael, pulling yet another angel cake from his backpack.

'Lovely,' said Jack.

The three friends went and sat in the summerhouse and chatted over a brew.

'Room for one more?' The voice came from behind them.

'Ee, our Gabriel! Aye Lad. Come and join us. Cake?' said Michael.

'Don't mind if I do.' Gabriel took a slice.

Jack went to get his additional guest a mug and a plate from the back kitchen and then the four of them chatted.

'All our troops are gathered near the Withy Grove ...'

Gabriel started.

'Withy Grove?' asked Godfrey

'Yes, the willow tree Sophia created down there has already reproduced itself and the lane down to the Irwell is now bordered by willow trees. Some of our angels have been weaving the withy stems into baskets to collect the abundance of fruit down there. So they started calling the lane the Withy Grove.'

'Go on,' said Godfrey, listening intently.

As Gabriel told them of all the other preparations, the sky turned cloudy, and it started to rain. The four friends chatted excitedly about the coming event as they drank more tea and had more angel cake.

'Righto,' said Michael. 'Me and our Gabriel will fly down to the place of Man and await your arrival.'

'Good plan,' said Jack.

The angels stepped from the summerhouse and unfurled their wings.

'Cheerio then,' winked Michael, and they were up and away, and soon disappeared from view.

'Right, Jack. We'd better be going too. I'll just use the facilities first,' said Godfrey.

Jack pushed his fingers through his hair, which still had some sawdust in it from that morning's carpentry. The rain turned to fine drizzle.

'We may need these,' said Godfrey, coming out of Jack's house holding a pair of bright yellow raincoats.

'Aye I think we will, Dad.'

The two figures climbed onto the tandem, Jack taking the front seat.

'Five! Four! Three! Two! ...'

'Can we just get on with it, son?'

'One! Blast off!' The two figures wobbled through the grounds of Jack's estate to the border of the heath at Newton. The heath had been transformed by Sophia and the increase in rainfall, since Godfrey and Anak had turned and broken the stopcock.

'Dad, you may need to turn the rainfall down a bit. I don't think it is set quite right,' said Jack, wiping his wet hair from his face.

'Bit of a story about that, son,' said Godfrey. 'I'm afraid Anak and I broke the tap. So, for now at least, we are stuck with it set a bit high.'

'Oh dear. We'll be getting webbed feet!' said Jack.

They reached Newton Lane (which ran where Oldham Road is now) and carried on down towards Ancoats, on the edge of the place of Man. Jack purposely aimed at big puddles and lifted his legs off the pedals as the bike splashed through.

'That were a big 'un, Dad!' he laughed.

Godfrey, a tad moist on the back seat, was quiet. He was pondering again.

4

Opposition

Not far from where Godfrey was creating the place of Man, there was a wild and lonely ley, as they used to call them – a woodland clearing. The country around the ley was desolate. It was a dark place and a black cloud hung over it every day since the rebellion. It drizzled constantly there. As a result, the clearing was covered in a dark green moss. And in the middle of the clearing was a clough – a very steep sided valley. Creatures who wandered near to the clough often got trapped on the slimy moss, and slipped down the black hole, where they became a meal for the residents.

At over a mile deep, this clough at the black ley, or Blackley as the locals called it, was actually an underground castle and the resident of this castle was Owd Hob, the king of the boggarts.

On this dark cold night, every boggart under Owd Hob's control was there, accompanied by their wives. Many Jack o' lanterns also gathered there – tall thin creatures dressed in grey suits with heads like pumpkins, and triangle eyes that flickered with candlelight. In the main hall of the underground castle, Owd Hob addressed his boggart army, and other dark creatures, in preparation for another war. These creatures had all been angels formerly. But, led by Owd Hob, they had risen up in rebellion and tried to overthrow Godfrey. Ever since that day, their appearance had begun to change. Disconnected from Godfrey, the light of life went out of them. Boggarts can transform themselves to look like anything, but in their natural state their skin is like that of a slug, and their eyes like bloodshot saucers. Their hair is green and their teeth are yellow.

Owd Hob talked about a world ruled by boggarts, but in reality he was the dictator of this dark kingdom. He had given each of the assembled creatures their evil powers and they knew he could take them back at any time.

He sat on a stone throne next to his wife Jinny. She was the boggart queen, and she sat smiling.

'My dear comrades,' began Owd Hob. 'Your presence here tonight gives me hope! Since we banded together, many winters ago, to overthrow the evil Godfrey and his oppressive rule, significant advances have been made. We now entirely control this black ley. Our clough, and this underground castle, are impenetrable. Most of the creatures Godfrey created no longer speak, at least not to him. Our strategy of steal, kill, and destroy is taking hold. My friends, the time has come for us to take full control of this world.'

The crowd applauded.

'When I am in power, the destruction of Godfrey-lovers will be my first and most important job. As soon as I have power, I shall have gallows after gallows erected; for example, in Salford and Old Trafford, on the vast fields there – as many of them as we can find space for. Then the Godfrey-lovers will be hanged one after another. We will dismember them and eat some of their flesh and drink their blood. And any remains will stay hanging until they stink. They will stay hanging as long as hygienically possible. As soon as they are untied or eaten, then the next group will follow. And that will continue until the last Godfrey-lover in Manchester is exterminated. Exactly the same procedure will be followed in other places until this land is cleansed of every last one of them!'

As the few candles flickered deep down in the boggart hole, cheers and applause filled the damp, dark air.

'Long live Owd Hob! Long live Owd Hob!' shouted the boggarts and Jack o' Lanterns. Owd Hob's wife, Jinny, smiled and nodded in agreement.

Owd Hob folded his arms and drank in the adulation of the gathered crowd.

'I have called you here tonight to tell you of a secret plot, by Godfrey himself, to usurp our kingdom and our power. Not content with disturbing our darkness with his light, he has an evil plan to reproduce himself! To multiply creatures that will look like him and sound like him. The arrogance of that hermit! I charge every creature of darkness here today to destroy his new idea before it takes root.

Our forces are, at this very moment, tunnelling underground to his new garden. We have developed the perfect weapon to undermine Godfrey's plan. Right now, the seed of the Cancer Tree is being planted.

This will be a new era of abundant food for us! Every Godfrey-lover who touches the tree will begin to die that very day. Where he plants life, we shall plant death! As more and more creatures die we shall have an abundance of flesh to eat, and blood to drink. No longer will we have to grow the moss-covered traps to capture our prey. They will die themselves and we will feast on their flesh in the dark hours!

Though we may be unable to overthrow Godfrey himself, let us work together in unity to steal, kill and destroy everything that is dear to him. If we are unrelenting in this task, we will eventually break his heart. And once we break his heart we will break his spirit more easily. And then the kingdoms of Manchester and Lancashire shall be ours!'

'Steal! Kill! Destroy! Steal! Kill! Destroy! Long live Owd Hob! Long live Hob!' shouted the boggarts and Jack o' lanterns again. Queen Jinny smiled and nodded again. She stroked the black cat on her lap - the only creature ever to survive falling into the boggart hole. She liked its darkness.

5

Albert and Edna

The smell of bacon wafted through the evening air in a large beautiful meadow not far from the end of Deansgate. Here and there, now the rain had finally stopped, angels cooked bacon butties over small camp fires. Every one of them on the planet had camped out in the meadow for that day's special event; white tents as far as the eye could see.

Eric, a junior angel, stood at the top of the meadow that day, looking towards Ancoats and awaiting the arrival of Godfrey and Jack. Soon, across the open fields towards Newton Lane , Eric saw two figures approaching on a tandem. He lifted his golden angel telescope to his eye to check it was them.

'Yes!' he said to himself. 'They are here!'

He collapsed his telescope and slipped it into his pocket. He lifted his golden trumpet to his lips, then pointed it towards Angel Meadow and gave three sharp blasts.

Cheers went up from the camp, and across the meadow angels stood to get a glimpse of the approaching pair.

Eric repeated the three blasts on his golden trumpet. Again the angels cheered.

'Holy! Holy! Holy!' shouted an angel in the crowd.

The rest of the angels responded. 'Oi! Oi! Oi!'

'Holy! Holy! Holy!' he shouted again.

'Oi! Oi! Oi!'

'Holy!'

'Oi!'

'Holy!'

'Oi!'

Then the chant was drowned out by cheers and whistles as Godfrey and Jack cycled into Angel Meadow. At the centre of the camp they were greeted by Michael and Gabriel, who had arrived some time ago.

A small table and four chairs had been arranged in the middle of the meadow and Michael and Gabriel sat and had a brew, and a bacon butty, with Godfrey and Jack.

After they had eaten and got their breath back, the four of them walked down the track, where Deansgate is today, towards Withy Grove. A procession of angels followed them. Some walked. Some hovered in the air to get a better view of Godfrey and Jack. As they approached the large willow tree near the River Irwell, the angels filed off and took up their positions around the border of the area. Every angel drew their golden sword.

Godfrey and Jack were smiling, looking at the

amazing garden Sophia had planted. There were flowers and fruits of every colour and size. Trees and small ponds punctuated the landscape. The place was brimming with life and a beautiful fragrance hung in the air. Godfrey could hardly believe that this was the place that had been so bleak and barren.

The River Irwell and the River Irk flowed with clear water. Myriads of brightly coloured fish swam in the waters. All sorts of birds called to one another from the treetops. There was nowhere else on earth so bustling and vibrant with new life.

Godfrey and Jack found Sophia sitting under the willow tree with tears in her eyes.

'Sophia, my love, what is the matter?' Godfrey asked.

Sophia didn't speak but pointed beyond the willow tree to another tree - a tree that somehow looked out of place. Godfrey and Jack went to inspect it.

'Oh no,' said Godfrey.

'What is it?' asked Jack.

'That, my son, is a Cancer Tree,' said Godfrey.

'Boggarts?' asked Jack.

'Boggarts,' said Godfrey.

He stroked his chin as he pondered some more.

'We've come too far to turn back now.'

'What's the plan now, Dad?'

'Hmm. I'm going to carry on and make man. We'll just have to warn them about this one tree.'

'Can't we destroy the Cancer Tree, Dad?'

Godfrey looked at Jack and his lip quivered and a tear began to well up in the corner of his eye.

'Jack please don't ask me to do that. You obviously don't know yet what that would involve.'

Godfrey hugged his son.

'Come on son. Let's get back to work.' Godfrey led Jack back to the willow tree. Jack didn't understand what his Dad meant. They came to where Sophia was sitting and Godfrey stooped down and wiped the tears from her eyes. 'It's going to be alright, Sophia.'

'I know,' she said. 'In the end, it will be.'

Godfrey took Sophia's hand and raised her up. The three of them walked towards the banks of the Irwell. On a bend in the river, near where Manchester Cathedral stands today, there was a sandy bank, like a small beach.

'Right, our Jack,' said Godfrey. 'You lie on the sand and stretch out your arms and legs like a starfish.'

Jack lay on his back on the sand as Godfrey had instructed. Godfrey knelt down and began to trace the shape of Jack onto the sand with his finger.

'No tickling now!' laughed Jack.

'Hold still, Jack. We need to get this right first time,' said Godfrey.

Once Jack's shape had been traced in the sand, Jack rolled over and knelt opposite Godfrey. The pair of them began to scoop sand into the shape until it became three-dimensional. They worked for over an hour, smoothing and adding fine detail as Sophia looked on. Finally they finished the sand sculpture and stood to admire their work.

'What do you think, Sophia?' Jack asked.

Sophia smiled as she looked at the shape on the ground.

'Right, Sophia, it is time. Let's do this,' said Godfrey.

Sophia closed her eyes for a moment and became very still. Then she opened her eyes again and knelt down beside the figure on the ground. She leaned in towards its head as though she was going to kiss it. Her lips touched his lips and she breathed out. Flesh began to appear, and bone and muscle. Eventually skin covered the man, and hair appeared on his head.

Sophia leaned back.

Godfrey sat by the creature for a moment to look at his face.

The eyes began to flicker and then they opened. The creature looked at the clouds in the sky for a moment and then suddenly sat up and looked around. 'Hang on a minute! What the 'eck's going on here?'

Godfrey looked him in the eye and smiled.

'Hello, Albert, I'm Godfrey.'

'Well pleased to meet you,' said Albert. 'But where the 'eck am I? What just happened?'

'It's alright my friend. I'll explain everything. Let's go for a walk.'

Godfrey helped Albert to his feet, and Albert began to walk, very slowly at first. He could not stop looking around at all the trees, and the birds, and the fish in the Irwell.

Godfrey and Albert walked in the cool of the day as Godfrey showed him around.

'All these trees have fruits that are delicious. So you can eat any you like. Oh, except one.'

Godfrey took Albert to the Cancer Tree.

'Now this one is poisonous, Albert. It really is

deadly. So don't even touch this one. All the rest are fine but if you eat anything off the Cancer Tree, you will die.'

'Righto. Everything's fine to eat except this one tree because it has deadly poisonous fruit. Right. I'll keep away from that one.'

They continued towards where Piccadilly Gardens are today. Sophia had planted a beautiful garden in that place, too. Outside Albert's new home a small pond continually bubbled with beef stew.

Godfrey and Albert found some dishes and spoons. Over dinner, the pair talked at length about many things as Albert had lots of questions.

'Are there other creatures like me?'

'There is no one like you Albert!' laughed Godfrey. But then he noticed that his answer brought a sort of sadness to Albert's face.

'What's wrong?'

'It'll be a bit blinkin' lonely on me own won't it?'

'But there are all the animals, birds and fish to enjoy.'

'Can they talk?'

'Well some of them still can. They all used to talk before the boggarts cast a spell on them.'

'Hmm. Not the same as having someone like me though is it?'

'Oh. I see,' said Godfrey, pondering again.

Albert yawned.

'Oh, what was that?' said Albert. 'It feels like all my energy is draining away.'

'Don't worry Albert. At the end of each day everything becomes still and sleeps. Even the sun in the sky rests for the night. But in a short time a new day will come and then your energy will return.'

'Oh I see,' said Albert, lying down. Soon he was asleep and gently snoring.

Godfrey heard someone approaching Albert's house. He went out to see Jack and Sophia coming towards him.

'How is he?' asked Jack. 'Must have been quite a shock!'

Godfrey stroked his chin and looked back towards Albert, who was now in a deep sleep.

'It's not good for man to be alone. Let us make him a friend, a partner. Someone he can share his life and love with. But let us not make this one identical. Let us make this partner more like Sophia than Jack.'

'That's a great idea, Dad.'

Sophia smiled. The three of them went into the room where Albert was sleeping. Sophia knelt beside Albert and closed her eyes for a moment.

She reached her hand into his side. She removed one of his ribs without Albert even stirring.

She turned to Godfrey and Jack, and all three of them held the rib.

'This one is not taken from his head to be over him. She is not taken from his foot to be under him. She is taken from his side to be with him.'

A bright light filled the room as Sophia began to sing the words she had just spoken.

When the light faded there before them stood a woman.

'What the 'eck was that? What's going on here?'

'Hello Edna,' said Godfrey, smiling and looking into

her eyes.

He explained about Albert and the new garden.

'Edna, soon you will fall asleep. Lie down near Albert and be still. In the morning, when the daylight comes, I will come and have breakfast with you. I'll explain more then.'

Edna soon felt drowsy and did as Godfrey suggested. She lay down near Albert and fell fast asleep.

As the sun began to set, Jack cycled back to his estate at Brookdale. Sophia ... well, she disappeared again as she often did. Like the wind, she blew here and there, often unseen. Godfrey walked back towards the willow tree at Withy Grove and spent the night on the banks of the Irwell. He looked up at the stars and pondered on the problem of the boggarts and the Cancer Tree. He really didn't want Albert and Edna to be dragged into all that old rebellion stuff.

Eventually, when the day was far spent, the gentle sound of the River Irwell flowing by made Godfrey drowsy, and he drifted into sleep.

6

The White Rat

Albert and Edna settled into the place of Man. Each day was like a glorious summer's day. They explored the garden Godfrey provided for them. One day they walked as far as Philip's Park – a beautiful estate where an angel called Philip lived. Philip was the head gardener at Jack's estate at Brookdale.

Philip made them a little picnic and took them on a tour of the grounds. They walked down to the River Medlock and sat on its sandy banks.

'Did you bring some water for a brew?' asked Albert.

Philip smiled.

'Today is a special day,' said Philip. 'Today I want you to taste something new.'

'What? We're not having a brew?' asked Edna concerned.

'Take these cups and dip them in the river,' said Philip.

'What? Just drink water? I was hoping for a brew,' complained Albert.

'Just try it. You'll be surprised,' said Philip.

Albert and Edna took their cups over to the river and dipped them in as Philip had instructed. They filled their cups and took a sip.

'Oh wow! What is that?' asked Albert.

'It's called lemonade,' said Philip.

'I love it! It's very sweet,' said Edna.

They scooped a few more cupfuls from the Medlock before sitting down with Philip to have some beef paste butties and the obligatory angel cake for dessert.

They laughed and told stories the whole afternoon. It was a lovely day and Philip was a fascinating angel. He was gentle and quiet - a very patient angel, who seemed old and wise. Maybe his patience had been learned while managing the large gardens on Jack's estate at Brookdale.

As the shadows lengthened and the busy world was hushed, Albert and Edna thanked Philip for a glorious afternoon and for introducing them to lemonade. As they were walking back towards their home near Piccadilly Gardens they heard a voice behind them.

'You going my way?' said the voice.

They turned round to see a white rat.

'Hope I didn't startle you.'

'No not at all,' said Albert. 'It's just that we keep forgetting that some of you animals can still talk.'

'Ah yes,' said the rat. 'That is very unfortunate. Anyway, my name is Reynard. Pleased to meet you.'

'Albert and Edna,' said Albert.

'Have you had a good afternoon?' asked Reynard.

Albert told him about their day and the wonderful discovery of the Medlock flowing with lemonade.

'Ah yes, there are many little secrets and surprises in this land Godfrey made. He's a bit of a joker you know. I never know if he is telling me the truth or just teasing me sometimes,' said Reynard.

'Oh I think he always tells the truth,' said Edna.

'Oh yes. I didn't mean anything by that. It's just that he likes to hide little surprises here and there, so we discover them unexpectedly. It's quite a hobby of mine, discovering the hidden secrets of Godfrey,' said Reynard.

'Really?' said Albert.

'Oh yes,' said Reynard. 'Have you found the little whisky waterfall hidden in Ancoats?'

'Whisky waterfall?' Albert asked.

'Oh I can show you. It's not far from here at all.'

Reynard led them to a small wooded hillside in Ancoats. In the middle of the woodland, what looked like a little waterfall was trickling down the rocks. Reynard pointed to the trickle.

'Have a sip of that,' he said.

Albert and Edna knelt down and caught some of the trickling liquid in their hands. They took a slurp and got the full effect of the whisky.

'Flippin' 'eck! That's got a kick!' said Albert.

Edna was clutching her throat.

'My throat's on fire!'

Reynard laughed.

'Ah yes. We only sip that stuff a little at a time. It's

not water or lemonade.'

As Reynard told them of other secret surprises hidden in creation, Albert and Edna became more and more impressed by their new friend.

Reynard took them on a little detour as they approached home.

'Let us pass by the Irwell, I want to show you a special treat there,' said Reynard.

Reynard scurried ahead to lead the way, and Albert and Edna followed. They arrived by the Irwell, near to the great willow tree at Withy Grove. Reynard led them a little further along the riverbank to the Cancer Tree.

'Have you tried the fruit from this tree?' asked Reynard.

'Oh no. That one is deadly poisonous,' said Albert. 'It'll kill you, that one will.'

'Who told you that?' asked Reynard.

'Godfrey,' said Edna. 'He told us to stay well clear of it, or we'll die.'

'You see, this is what I mean. Godfrey is teasing you,' said Reynard. 'You won't die if you eat this fruit. You'll actually start to develop magic powers like Godfrey.'

'Are you sure?' asked Edna.

'Yes I am sure,' said Reynard. 'We animals who still speak are able to do so because of this wonderful tree.'

'So we won't die then?' asked Albert.

'Of course you won't die! Do you think Godfrey is going to plant something deadly in this wonderful garden he made for you? Of course not! But like the whisky waterfall he has hidden other special treats he knows you'll discover as time goes on. I'm just giving you a shortcut so you can enjoy life more,' Reynard assured them.

'Well it does look very special. And the flowers smell beautiful,' said Edna. 'It doesn't look poisonous.'

'Go ahead. Just try a little bit,' said Reynard. 'If you don't like it, spit it out.'

'Well it can't do any harm I suppose,' said Edna.

'Look if you are worried, watch me.' Reynard ran up the tree and sniffed around for a ripe fruit. He kicked a few of the bright blue fruits off a branch and ran down again.

'Mmm! Smell that fruit!' said Reynard, and he bit into one of them. 'Delicious!'

Edna picked two of the fruits up and handed one to Albert.

'They do smell lovely don't they Albert?' she said.

'Aye they do,' said Albert, sniffing the fruit.

They both took little bites and were amazed by the wonderful taste. It was like nothing else they had tasted in the garden. Perhaps it was the effect of the whisky or it was just really amazing fruit, but it tasted wonderful. It produced a sort of euphoria and all three of them laughed.

'How could we have thought this was poisonous?' asked Albert.

'Ah, that Godfrey, he's a trickster,' said Reynard.

As they looked at Reynard, they noticed his fur became darker. The white fur was turning grey and then jet black. And then he seemed to grow bigger, and his laugh became more disturbing and mocking. Until there before them stood Owd Hob himself, laughing at them.

'You idiots! You fell for that one so easily!'

And off he went, laughing all the way back to Boggart Hole Clough.

Albert and Edna had never seen or heard of Owd Hob before and didn't really know what had just happened.

'We'll have to ask Godfrey about this,' said Albert with a half-eaten fruit in his hand.

The euphoria they had felt seemed to wear off all too quickly and they both began to get a headache and feel sick. A black cloud crept across the sky and the day became overcast. The birdsong stopped as the birds fell silent in the trees. As the couple sat under the Cancer Tree, they looked in

horror at the dead fish floating down the Irwell. The waters were turning grey and murky - no longer crystal clear.

All across the place of Man, beauty was slipping away. The Medlock turned from lemonade to muddy polluted water. The leaves of the trees lost life and dropped to the ground over the next few days. And once again, angel tears fell on the land.

In the distance they heard a voice calling them.

'Albert? Edna?' It was Godfrey.

'Oh no! What have we done Edna?' said Albert. Something they had never felt before filled their hearts – guilt, shame and fear.

'Quick, let's hide in the bushes!' she said.

The pair of them hid in the bushes near the Cancer Tree as Godfrey approached.

'Albert, where are you?' Godfrey asked, looking at the bushes.

'We're here, Godfrey, in the bushes,' said Albert,

realising it was pointless to hide.

'My question wasn't geographical, Albert,' said Godfrey. 'I know where you are. I always see you. I mean where are you in your heart? Where are we in our friendship? What have you done to the place of Man?'

'It wasn't me, Godfrey! It was Edna! She made me eat from the Cancer Tree!' said Albert.

'Hang on a minute you cheeky twonk!' said Edna. 'You were just as willing as I was. It wasn't us anyway Godfrey. A rat came and talked us into it. Reynard, his name was. But then he turned into this right ugly old bloke with green hair and yellow teeth!'

'Oh no!' said Godfrey. 'Owd Hob! This is terrible. Now instead of all the fruit and food you need, the land will require you to work very hard for it to produce anything. The pond of stew will become putrid and everything will be really hard work now. You have connected everything I have made to the Cancer Tree.

And you Edna, when you have children, it will be painful for you because that is the effect of this fruit on living things. It brings pain and toil and suffering.'

'Will we die then?' asked Albert.

'In one sense you already have, Albert,' said Godfrey. 'The pain in your head and your stomach, and the sickness in your body is death already, compared with what I planned for you. But yes, you will also die. Not today and not tomorrow, but death has taken hold of you. It will bring a great sadness – not only to you but to all your children.'

A tear fell down Godfrey's cheek. And even as he was speaking to them he seemed somehow to grow less visible and his voice harder to hear. Godfrey was there all right, and his voice had not really become quieter. It was the effect of the Cancer Tree – it made it difficult for Albert and Edna to see or hear him as clearly as before. It was their eyes and ears that had become dim.

On that day a deep sadness settled over the land. The deep sadness also settled in Albert's heart. He carried uneasiness in his chest that never went away. He wondered how life would have been, had he and Edna not eaten from the Cancer Tree.

Albert and Edna had many, many children. Life became hard, just as Godfrey had told them. Albert and his sons worked all day on their allotments to grow food for their families. Some of them hunted animals for food. The women wove clothes and cooked for the men when they came back from the allotment, or from hunting. Sometimes there were fights and disagreements. On one occasion, one man killed his own brother.

The garden Godfrey had planted for them became diseased; all the plants died and the pond of stew dried up.

They moved to settle nearer to the Irwell but their new home was never as good as the old one. In fact, it was a complete shambles.

The place became known as Manchest, because everyone knew of the deep sadness that Albert carried in his chest. That is why today it is known as Manchester.

If you go to that place today, you'll still find traces of the olden days. Withy Grove is there, named after the willow trees that lined the lane before the deep sadness came. The great rivers of the Irwell, the Irk and the Medlock are still there, though their waters are not clear anymore but dark and muddy. Even the Old Shambles

– Albert and Edna's second home – is still there too.

The broken stopcock at Woodhead was never fixed and that's why it rains so much in Manchester. But the Manchester drizzle – now that is something quite different. Every so often, angels gather at Angel Meadow, down near Victoria Station, and they reminisce about the days before the deep sadness. And after they break camp and go about their duties, they fly over Manchester and sometimes they cry, thinking about what could have been. And their gentle angel tears fall like drizzling rain, to shower a blessing of peace on the people of Manchester.

7

Norman builds a boat

Norman Atkinson lived in a ramshackle cottage on his farm in Clayton Vale. He was the many-times-great-great-grandson of Albert and Edna and he had been born over one thousand years after Albert had been created on the banks of the Irwell.

He awoke on this chilly autumnal day feeling a cold draught over his shoulder. His wife was still asleep by his side. It was still early and something seemed wrong about the start of this day.

Norman went downstairs to get a brew and discovered he'd had another break-in. The kitchen window was smashed and the frame was hanging from its twisted hinges. Food and other items were strewn across the kitchen. He went out of the back door and walked to a small vegetable patch at the end of his garden. The thieves had uprooted his prize marrow and destroyed all his hard work.

He walked back to the kitchen in sadness and recovered the kettle from the chaos and put it on the stove to make a brew. He too carried the deep sadness in his chest. But the deep sadness Norman carried was really about how dark and violent life had become. Crimes went unchecked. Murders were a daily occurrence. People were stealing, killing and destroying across the land. The light of Godfrey was fading from the world, and Owd Hob and the boggarts were rejoicing.

Norman's wife came downstairs and, with a depressing resignation to the constant break-ins, began to tidy up without saying a word. Norman fixed the hinges back on the window frame and taped up a bit of brown paper to keep the draft out. He drank his brew but was very uneasy.

'I'm going for a walk, Lass,' he said to Mrs Atkinson.

'OK, Love,' she said, spreading a little jam on a slice of bread.

Norman wandered down the bank of the River Medlock as far as Berry Brow. He turned up the hill, on this day, and walked to Bluebell Woods. Lost in his thoughts about the constant criminality in Manchester, he also got lost in the woods.

A high wall at the edge of the woods jolted him out of his musings. He followed the line of the wall for a while, imagining the old days before the Cancer Tree ruined everything. He longed for the day when Godfrey could be seen and heard again. This was the desire of his heart - something to bring hope and light to the world once more.

Just ahead he noticed something– a narrow gate hidden in a recess in the wall. "Come in. All are welcome" read some faded lettering, hand-painted on the gate. Curious as to where it led, he tried the handle.

The gate opened with ease. He listened for a moment but all he could hear was the cooing of a woodpigeon in the distance. He hoped he wasn't trespassing or anything. Creeping through some rhododendron bushes, he found a little track, which led to a small stream. There, by the stream, was another hand-painted sign.

"Cross the stream and come up to the house for food and chats! All welcome."

There was lightness and peace in this place that Norman had never known. He took off his shoes and socks and paddled across the stream. He was so taken with the beauty of the place he forgot to put his socks and shoes on when he reached the other side.

The track opened out into a formal garden with flower beds and manicured lawns. In the distance, Norman spotted a large white house. This must belong to the owner who invites us for "food and chats" thought Norman. The peacocks squawked on the lawns and Norman walked up towards the white mansion open-mouthed.

'Ay up!' said a voice behind Norman.

Norman turned round but couldn't see anyone.

'Down here, Lad!' laughed the stranger. It was Philip, the angel, who was planting some fresh bedding plants for the autumn season.

'I do hope I am not trespassing!'

'Not at all Lad! They've been expecting you.'

'They?'

'Yes. Godfrey and Jack have been preparing a lovely lunch for you since breakfast time. They are really looking forward to eats and chats.'

'They are?'

'Yes. Just go towards the house. They'll come and meet you.'

Norman walked nervously up the drive. When he was still far off, Godfrey spotted him and ran to meet him.

'Norman! My dear man,' said Godfrey, giving Norman a hug so big it made him feel a little awkward.

'Norman, you wonderful man! You found the narrow gate then? Of course you did! Why are you carrying your shoes, Lad? They all seem to do that,' chuckled Godfrey. 'Come up to the house and take the weight off.'

Norman, still slightly dazed at meeting Godfrey, and being able to see and hear him very clearly, didn't know what to make of all this.

'Come in! Come in!' said Godfrey, motioning towards the open conservatory door. 'This is my son, Jack.'

'Welcome, Norman,' said Jack. 'Beef stew for lunch today!'

'Oh th-thank yyou ...' stuttered Norman.

As they sat down to lunch, served by Eric, the junior angel, Jack explained that the stew was made to the recipe of the stew that used to cook itself in Albert's stew pond, before the deep sadness.

'Claret?' said Godfrey, pouring a small glass to have with the meal.

'Now, Norman, we drew you here today because we have a mission for you,' began Jack.

'Yes,' said Godfrey. 'We want you to build a boat.'

'A boat?' asked Norman.

'Aye, and a flippin' humongous one at that!' said Jack.

And so, as Norman tried to take in this amazing place and its inhabitants, Godfrey and Jack explained the serious situation. Boggarts had infected most of the population with a destructive self-centredness and a disregard for every other human. Violence and crime filled the whole land. But now the boggarts had one last plan - to do serious damage to one of the climate controls and flood the whole earth, killing every living thing but themselves.

'Norman, you and your family are the only ones left who have a heart towards light and life,' said Godfrey. 'You are the only ones who seek to hear our voice or see our face. Today we have answered that prayer. We want you to build this vessel to save your family and some of the animals, so we can start again after Jack and I overthrow Owd Hob's plan of complete destruction.'

Godfrey handed Norman a rolled-up plan of the humongous boat.

'And don't worry. Jack is a carpenter and he will be with you from time to time to whisper guidance in your ear during the construction.'

'Aye, that I will,' said Jack.

Two hours later and Norman was paddling through the stream, on his way home. He dried his feet, put his shoes and socks back on and followed the track through the rhododendron bushes to the narrow gate. He walked slowly home, pondering what a strange day it had been.

It took three days for Mrs Atkinson to come round to

the idea of building a huge boat in Clayton Vale, when it was miles from the sea. But on the second night after Norman broke the news of his meeting with Godfrey and Jack, she had a nightmare about the flood engulfing the whole land. After a family meeting the next day, Norman's three sons and their wives all committed themselves to the task. They spent the next month in Bluebell Woods, felling trees for the task and sawing and transporting them back to Clayton Vale.

As the huge structure took shape, Norman was repeatedly mocked by people from neighbouring farms. They thought he was quite mad. The last few days were spent gathering food supplies and painting the vessel with tar inside and out.

Just as promised, when only Norman was working on it, Jack had appeared and helped him with the task.

Godfrey had walked down to Clayton Vale and instructed Norman to get his family aboard the craft and live on it.

One evening, a cool wind blew from the East. As the family stood on deck looking at the landscape, they heard a strange sound. In the distance they saw Godfrey singing– he was calling for Sophia. A bright light began to appear from within the ship. Then they knew Sophia was with them. As her presence grew stronger, slowly, from all directions, birds began to arrive in couples– Ospreys took up residence in the eaves of the ship's roof. Horses, goats and sheep also arrived in pairs. All through the night, and from as far away as Yorkshire, animals came to the ark. By two o'clock in the morning, exotic animals had arrived – elephants, giraffes, lions and tigers. It began to rain.

In the darkness of Woodhead Valley, some boggarts had found the mains water pipe that controlled the rainfall for all of Manchester and beyond. They thought it would be funny to burst the pipe, so they dropped huge boulders onto it, levered it with tree branches and jumped on them until finally it burst. 'At last!' they said, 'The whole of Godfrey's creation will be destroyed! Every man will die, and their wives and children!' The boggarts ran off laughing and headed to Blackley to tell Owd Hob the good news.

As a result, all control was lost of the surrounding rivers and the rainfall. Rivers immediately began to burst their banks and a head of water was building down the Irwell, the Irk and the Medlock.

Rain like a monsoon began to fall without any respite. By six o'clock in the morning the Medlock Valley was a massive lake. Norman had closed the doors of the ark at about four o'clock– when the last animals had taken up residence. The ark was now afloat and less and less land was visible.

The rain continued for forty days and forty nights without any let up. The family lived alongside the animals, as the ark creaked and listed from side to side. By the end of the month, even the Mountains of Ninepence had been engulfed by the waters, and no land was visible in any direction. Norman and his family were kept busy feeding the animals and shovelling vast amounts of animal poop over the side of the ark into the water.

Every now and then they would see several dead bodies floating in the water. Death seemed to be all around them, but the ark of Godfrey and the presence of Sophia kept Norman and his family safe.

'You know, all this death is terrible,' said Norman to Mrs Atkinson as they stood on the deck one evening watching the sunlight fade. 'But, in a way, it could be a good thing – a cleansing, a fresh start for the whole world. Maybe this dark event will turn out for good – to bring a new hope and light to the world.'

'Maybe it will, Love. But will we ever get over the sorrow?'

'Who knows, Lass?' said Norman.

After forty days, the rain finally stopped. The ark continued to drift along, pulled by currents and winds. Without any landmarks Norman had no idea where they were until one morning, it dawned on him...

'Get one of them there canaries and let's release it. If it doesn't come back we'll know it has found dry land.'

Mrs Atkinson caught a canary and handed it to Norman. He went up on deck and released the bird. It flew off and then returned a few minutes later. It did this several times and then Norman caught it and put it back in the ark with its mate. She didn't find dry land.

'Another week of shovelling animal poop overboard it seems,' said Norman.

A week later he thought he'd let a budgie have a go. She flew off and was gone quite a while. But she returned with a buttercup in her beak.

'Oh, good news Mrs Atkinson!' shouted Norman. 'She's found dry land.'

The ark continued to drift until small islands were spotted more frequently. At the end of the week, in the early hours of the morning, the whole family were woken up by a sudden thud. They came out onto the deck to discover they had grounded near Gorton. They looked across the landscape where trees and vegetation were already thriving. The darkness of the previous world seemed to have been washed away. Everything was made new.

'What a beautiful view,' said Norman.

From that day the spot where the ark came to rest became known as Beautiful View – although these days it is called 'Bellevue'.

Norman wanted to be a good steward of this new chance Godfrey had given them. So he got his three sons– Shane, Harry and Joseph– to build pens for all the animals so they could breed in captivity and not be wiped out by some evil boggart's antics. And there the family lived for the rest of their days, managing the animals at Bellevue Zoo and gradually releasing the animals' offspring into the wild until the world was once again filled with creatures.

The zoo stayed in the family for years, managed by Mrs Atkinson and the sons. Norman, it is said, had a bit of a breakdown and began to drink heavily. Some said it was what we now call 'survivor guilt' – he was overcome with a sense of unworthiness at having survived the mass extinction of men and women. Others said he became obsessed with the vineyard he had planted after the flood. He became less and less interested in the animals, and more and more interested in creating fine wines. And the more he drank and got drunk, the less he was able to hear the voice of Godfrey, until the day when that journey, through the narrow gate to Jack's mansion, became a distant memory and some days it felt to him like it had only been a dream.

Somehow, just like his ancestors, Albert and Edna, Norman seemed to let go of his friendship with Godfrey and became increasingly entangled in the temptations that the boggarts put in his path. He ended his days getting drunk every day and sleeping naked on the bed in the afternoons. Mrs Atkinson often cried as the deep sadness took root in her heart.

8

The Tower of Blackpool

Long after the days of Norman and his floating zoo, there was a hardware shop at Blackpool owned by a man called Terry. *'Terry's Hardware'* was the unimaginative name of the shop. Terry's son Alan worked in the shop and had recently become a partner, as trade was doing very well due to a large building project nearby.

The people of Blackpool had decided to build a tower that reached up to the sky. The amount of nuts and bolts and screws and whatnots the builders required made owning a hardware store in that place extremely profitable. Every day the builders came to Terry's Hardware and asked Alan for all sorts of size six thin-gamabobs and size eight whatnots. Alan's nephew Len was hired during this time to help in the shop.

There, by the sea, the tower took shape. Every day the people came to look at the progress. But there weren't enough builders for the job. They sent out messages everywhere saying there was plenty of work for builders, engineers and labourers while the tower was being built.

Soon workers came from everywhere. Some even came across from Poland, France and Germany. In fact, too many workers came. And now they had trouble understanding each other. All sorts of arguments broke out. There was confusion about whether measurements were in imperial or metric, and the whole project floundered for quite some time. Eventually, the workers from over the water got fed up and returned to their lands. The Lancashire workers continued the building work, but at a much slower pace.

One evening, Alan took his dog for a walk on the deserted beach. He saw someone approaching and thought he recognised them. The person seemed to be glowing as he got nearer. When Alan recognised the stranger he knelt on the sand before him. It was Godfrey.

Godfrey lifted him back up to his feet.

'Alan, how you doing, Lad?'

'We're doing really well at our shop with the tower construction and all that.'

'Alan, I have come to tell you that we have chosen you to be a new beginning for the people of the North West; to be like a new Albert or a new Norman. But it won't work here. You'll need to get your things together, you and Susan, and travel towards Manchester to a place I will show you. There in that place I will bless you and you will be a blessing to others. To you and your descendants I will give the lands of Manchester and Lancashire.'

This last bit of the promise troubled Alan, as he and Susan couldn't have children. How could Godfrey speak of his descendants while they were childless?

Soon Alan was aware of other figures standing by Godfrey's side. He thought he saw Jack, and then a lady glowing with life and colour.

Suddenly they were gone. Alan looked around but he was alone with his dog, who was now straining on the lead towards the sea.

Alan walked back slowly that night and wondered about the visitation. As Susan cooked them some cod and chips, Alan told her about the visitation. The pair slept peacefully and woke in the morning with a conviction that they should do what Godfrey had said.

'We must be mad!' said Susan over breakfast. 'Leaving here and going to Manchester. What will it be like?'

'It'll be like a fresh start,' said Alan. 'An adventure with Godfrey!'

Though they were excited by the new adventure, Alan's Dad, Terry, was not because Len, Alan's nephew, said he was going as well. This left Terry with no one to work in the shop, which had been in the family for generations.

But Alan and Susan stood firm, and a few weeks later they loaded their belongings onto a horse and cart and set off towards Manchester, with their nephew Len and his wife, Edith. The four of them had a couple of tents on the cart and they camped along the way– at Preston the first night and then Bolton the next night.

On the third day as they were approaching Salford, Alan became restless.

'What's wrong Alan?' asked Susan.

'I'm just thinking, Love. I hear these Salford types can be very rough. They fight each other to win good-looking girls y' know. I don't like fighting. You are stunning; they may look at you and decide to do me over so they can have you. I wonder if it would be safer for us all if we just tell them you are my sister.'

'Well if you think that is best, Love.'

'I think it will help us avoid unnecessary trouble, that's all.' After a few days at Salford they found a place to rent, and Alan and Susan, and Len and his wife, moved in. They waited for Godfrey to show up and give them the next set of directions. Days passed. Alan opened a hardware stall on Salford market, with some stock he'd brought with him. He had plenty of money as he had taken his half of his father's business when he left Blackpool. But he wanted to start trading as soon as possible because that is what he did. Susan helped on the market stall and men often visited– not to buy hardware, just to have a look at Susan. She was gorgeous.

Eventually, news of her beauty reached the Mayor of Salford. And one Saturday morning he called by the stall to ask if they had half a dozen four-inch countersunk slot head screws.

'I think we can find you some of those,' said Susan, fluttering her eyelids at the enchanted Mayor. 'Would you like anything else?' The Mayor blushed and smiled.

Before long, Susan was dining at Salford Town Hall in the Mayor's private quarters. Quite how that happened Alan and Susan were unsure, except that the Mayor was quite a charming and friendly man and, in order to keep up the pretence that Susan was Alan's sister, they had run out of excuses as to why she shouldn't go for dinner.

After dessert and coffee had been served, the Mayor

told the servants that would be all for the night. He walked over to the French doors that opened onto the Garden and invited Susan to walk with him. The night air was warm and the clear starlit sky was magnificent. The birds could be heard settling down for the night at Peel Park. The moonlight only served to make Susan look more beautiful than ever.

The Mayor took Susan in his arms and embraced her. He kissed her - gently at first and then passionately.

'Stop! Stop!' Susan protested, pushing the Mayor away.

'My Dear! What is wrong? Have I offended you in some way?'

'No. No. You have been the perfect gentleman. You have courted me, complemented me, wined and dined me. You have been perfect. It is I who have offended you, Mr Mayor! My husband and I have lied to you and everyone! We are not brother and sister. We are husband and wife.'

'What? Why did you do that?'

'Alan thought the men here would do him over to get me.'

'What? We are not barbarians here in Salford you know! We have self-respect.'

The Mayor called in the chauffeur, who prepared the official horse and carriage and sent Susan back to Alan, who was waiting nervously for her return.

'We've been busted!' she told him. They didn't sleep much that night wondering what would happen.

At 8am there was a loud banging on their door.

'You crook! You complete git! You lying little scumbag!' blurted the Mayor, stepping through the door and pinning Alan to the wall.

'Do you have any idea what you have done? No. You actually don't do you?'

'I have been the Mayor of Salford for twenty years. Do you know why, Alan? It is because I have been unlike most politicians round here. I have built trust through acting with integrity. Do you know what integrity is, Alan? No, you don't. You don't know what it is. You are happy to lie and cheat your way through life aren't you? If Susan had not come clean last night, if I had proposed to her and announced my marriage to her – as I intended to do – and then this had been discovered – I'd have been finished, Alan! The end of my long unblemished career in local politics because you, you little Godfrey-lover, were happy to lie!'

A vein began to throb in the Mayor's forehead and his left eye began to twitch. Alan could not recall ever seeing anyone quite as angry as this.

'You have twenty-four hours, Alan. If you and your stupid family are still in Salford in twenty-four hours, I'll have all four of you arrested and thrown into jail. Pack your stuff and leave now!' The Mayor pushed Alan to the floor before storming out of the lodging place. Alan shook with fear and Susan burst into tears.

At midnight, having carefully explained the situation to Len and Edith – using a few more half-truths to make himself look good, Alan persuaded the four of them to get back on the road and head for Manchester.

9

Blood and stars

As they travelled through the darkness, Alan and Len kept each other company as Susan and Edith slept. The horse was weary, and Alan and Len were not really concentrating on navigation. Alan just wanted to escape the shouting Mayor of Salford.

In the early hours of the morning the horse lurched towards the riverbank of the Irwell close to where Albert had been created many years before and stooped to drink the water.

'Let's camp here for the night,' said Alan to Len.

Len got to work erecting the small cover they had for the cart, without waking the sleeping ladies.

Soon all were asleep except Alan. He sat on the bank of the Irwell feeling bad about lying to the people of Salford. He had fallen out with his Dad in Blackpool, and then he'd fallen out with his new neighbours in Salford. Maybe he should have stayed in Blackpool, he thought to himself. He wanted to trust Godfrey on this adventure. It was just that he thought Godfrey needed a bit of help in bringing things about. Godfrey tended to be a bit slow, whereas Alan was a salesman, eager to close every deal.

As he was having his little pity party with himself, he noticed a light on the water. Was it the moonlight dancing on the Irwell? No. This was something else. He saw a figure in green dungarees walking on the water towards him. As the stranger drew closer, it looked like three figures.

'Hello, Alan,' said Godfrey. Alan was struggling to make out the other two figures.

'Don't be afraid. I am your protection and your reward. I am giving this land to your descendants. From the Mountains of Ninepence all the way to Warrington.'

'Forgive me, Godfrey ...' said Alan. 'My descendants? You know full well Susan is not able to have children. How then shall I have any descendants at all?'

Godfrey raised Alan to his feet and put his arm around his shoulder. He led him a short way away from the horse and cart and his sleeping family.

'How many stars are in the sky tonight Alan?'

'Erm ... One. Two ...' began Alan, but then realised he could not number them.

'There are too many to count,' said Alan.

Godfrey looked him in the eye.

'So shall be the number of your descendants in this land.' A sort of thud hit Alan's chest. That place where Alan held the deep sadness was assaulted with the power of Godfrey's promise. The sadness eased as Alan looked up at the stars. A tear fell from his eye. He somehow knew in that moment that he would be a father one day.

'Who's the Daddy?' asked Godfrey.

'What?' said Alan.

'Who's the Daddy?' repeated Godfrey.

'Oh ... Erm.. I'm the Daddy ...' said Alan, as he embraced the promise.

'On this night, here by the Irwell, I am making an agreement with you,' said Godfrey. 'All that I am, I give to you. All that I have, I share with you, in love. Everything I have is yours. And everything you have is mine.'

Another tear rolled down Alan's face.

Godfrey reached into his pocket and pulled out a golden penknife. He winked at Alan.

He opened his own hand and cut a line across his thumb. The line turned red with blood. He took Alan's hand and opened it.

'OK?' asked Godfrey.

'Yes,' gulped Alan incredulously.

Godfrey took the penknife and cut a line across Alan's thumb. The line turned red with blood.

Godfrey pushed the bleeding thumbs together.

'We are now one blood, Alan. You are mine and I am yours. One forever. And in this joining of man and Godfrey, all the people of this kingdom will be blessed. This is an everlasting agreement,' he said.

He hugged Alan and smiled. 'All will be well. And all will be well.'

Alan was a bit overwhelmed and felt tired. He was vaguely aware that Godfrey and the other two figures were floating away over the waters of the Irwell. Alan lay down on the bank of the Irwell and looked up at the starlit sky. He pondered about having children, about having numerous descendants, and how he would mention this to Susan.

And quietly, as he pondered the day's events, he drifted into sleep right there on the riverbank.

10

The surrogate affair

Alan woke next morning with the dog licking his face. He had fallen asleep on the bank of the Irwell, thinking about the promises of Godfrey. Susan came along and found him.

'What the 'eck did you sleep there for?' she asked.

'You won't believe what happened last night,' said Alan.

They lit a small fire and got a brew on, and some breakfast on the go, as Alan told Susan all about the vision of Godfrey. He showed her the wound on his thumb where he and Godfrey had sealed the promise with their blood.

Susan found it hard to imagine that she would be a mother, after all the years of it just being the two of them. In one sense, Len, their nephew, had been like a surrogate son, as he had always spent more time with Alan than his own dad.

The four of them settled into Manchester and opened a hardware shop on Shudehill. Business was good and they always made a good profit. After a year or so, Len decided to go into business on his own, and opened his own shop on Ancoats Street about a mile away. When Len left Alan's shop, Susan had to help out and became overworked– looking after both the house and the shop. So Alan and Susan decided to advertise for a lodger who could help in the shop or do the housework. A few days later a young girl named Helen came to ask about the vacancy and subsequently took up lodging in the spare room above the shop. Summers and winters passed but Susan did not become pregnant. One day she suggested an idea to Alan.

'This baby is not coming, Alan,' began Susan. 'I wonder if the answer is staring us right in the face. What about asking Helen to carry a child for us? We could pay her for it.'

'What? You mean conceive a baby through Helen? How would you feel about that?'

'Well obviously, it is far from perfect. But if Godfrey told you that you would be a father when we settled here, then that is what must happen by any means.'

Alan was unsure about the idea but Helen was very attractive and considerably younger than Susan. He didn't think the idea was entirely without merit. He left Susan to broach the subject with Helen.

Helen was against the idea at first but, when Susan offered her a considerable sum of money, she finally agreed to become a surrogate mother for them. Susan went away for a weekend and left Alan and Helen in the house together. They never talked about what happened that weekend but a few months later Helen found that she was pregnant.

When Helen realised she was expecting Alan's baby something changed. She began to look down on Susan and despise her. She began to daydream that she was more desirable than Susan because she was expecting. She wondered if she could replace Susan and marry Alan, who was now extremely wealthy. The more she flirted with Alan the more Susan became angry. Then, one rainy day, the women had a huge argument and Susan threw Helen's belongings out of the upstairs window.

'Get out you whore!' Susan yelled.

'Don't worry you old cow. I was leaving anyway!' shouted Helen.

The pregnant Helen gathered her few belongings and walked off in the rain. She was so hurt and angry that, by that afternoon, she had walked all the way to Failsworth. Unfamiliar with the area, she found herself walking through Bluebell Woods where the leaves of the trees formed a canopy that sheltered her. She put a blanket on the ground and covered herself with her spare clothes and fell asleep.

At first light she woke to the sound of someone whistling. The smell of bacon was in the air. She peered round the side of the tree to see Jack cooking over a fire. A kettle was coming to the boil and a teapot and two cups were standing by.

'Lovely morning!' said Jack, winking in her direction. 'Bacon butty and a brew, Chuck, that's what you need.'

'Thank you,' said Helen, trying to straighten her just-woke-up-hair.

'Now Helen, you're Susan's housekeeper at the hardware shop aren't you? So what are you doing in these distant parts?'

Helen explained the whole situation to Jack and he

listened sympathetically. He served up the bacon butties and poured a brew for them both. As Helen confessed her pregnancy she burst into tears, fearing that the baby would have a hopeless start.

'Hey, come on, Lass,' said Jack, putting a friendly arm around her and wiping her tears away.

'You are pregnant and you'll have a son. He will become the head of a great family. We don't make any accidental children, you know. Every child born has a purpose. Now today, when you have straightened yourself up, go back to Susan and apologise. She will take you back. She's feeling really bad about what happened because it was her idea in the first place.'

'Are you serious?' asked Helen.

'I am Helen. Why? What alternate plans do you have? Live in the wood here and let the child be brought up by boggarts?' smiled Jack.

'How do you know all these things? How do you know my name?' asked Helen.

'I always see you Helen. My Dad and I see everyone. It is just the eyes and ears of humans that have become dim. When people are desperate, sometimes their vision clears and they can see us again. That is why I am so clear to you now.'

Jack helped Helen pack her things and walked her as far as Oldham Road. He gave her a hug as they parted.

'Go on, Lass. It'll be all right.'

And, as true as Jack's word, it was all right. When Helen got back to the shop, Alan and Susan apologised for putting her in such a difficult position. Helen apologised for flirting with Alan. And although the truce was a tense one, it did endure. The baby was born – a little boy – and they called him Malcolm.

And just one year later, Susan discovered she too was pregnant and gave birth to a son. They called him Ian, and he became the head of a very large family in Manchester, just as Godfrey had promised.

As both boys grew up, they were always fighting and, as Malcolm was a year or so older than Ian, he usually won. This caused arguments between the two women and also broke Alan's heart, as both boys were his sons.

In the end, Helen decided to leave Manchester, taking Malcolm with her. She felt it was for the best. This time they tried to make the parting more amicable but nevertheless permanent. She travelled to Oldham and settled there. She never saw Alan or Susan again.

Alan and Susan became known as the two pensioners with a pushchair, due to having a child so late in life. They were well known at that time all across Manchester.

Malcolm grew up in Oldham not really knowing who his father was. And every time Alan put little Ian on his lap and played with him, his thoughts turned to Malcolm and how life was for him. He never discussed this pain with Susan because she never wanted what had happened to be mentioned in the family ever again. So, embracing this strange and dysfunctional situation, they lived their lives above the hardware shop at Shudehill near the Irwell.

11

The Barbecue

Martin Simmonite was born into violence, famine and poverty. He was a few weeks old when his mother stood in the crowd at the Manchester Massacre. Tensions ran high at St Peter's Field as a debate raged about the national government. The crowd was very large but unarmed and peaceful. Martin's mother stood with her neighbour in the crowd. She also had a two-year-old babe in her arms. As the cavalry charged into the crowd with sabres drawn, his mother's friend was knocked down by a charging horse. Her baby fell from her arms and suffered a severe head injury. He died a few moments later. He was the first victim of the massacre.

The unrest of the poor at that time was great, and Martin witnessed many skirmishes, fights and battles as he grew up.

On his twentieth birthday, he had been drinking in a pub in Ancoats till the late hours, with his brother Arthur and some friends. On their way home they met a group of drunken Italian immigrants, who were looking for a fight. He tried to encourage his friends to avoid the fight and not be drawn into violence. Then one of the Italians began beating his brother Arthur severely. He tried to break up the fight but the Italian man was having none of it. The fight turned nasty and Martin pinned him to the ground, repeatedly punching him in the face until he stopped fighting and went limp. Martin looked down at the man and saw blood oozing from his ears. His own blood ran cold. He realised he had killed the man. Suddenly all his instinct was to flee from the scene. It was only the chaos of the fight that prevented the Italians from noticing that their friend was dead.

Martin jumped up and pushed through the melee. He saw a dark alleyway leading into a maze of slum dwellings in Ancoats. He ran as fast as he could. No one noticed his escape until much later. He began to head for home but then realised that the Italians would get his identity from one of his friends and come round to execute him for the killing.

He turned down another alleyway and headed towards open countryside. He ran ...

and walked ...

and walked ...

and ran, until he was far, far away.

He wasn't sure what his wife and children would think when he failed to return home. But fear took him prisoner that night and he didn't see them or his brother again for forty years.

o0o

The distant hum of the angel Philip mowing the lawns of Brookdale Park was the perfect soundtrack to this gorgeous summer's day. Godfrey and Sophia were sitting under the shade of a small willow tree just outside the white mansion. Sophia was reading a history book about Anak's Castle at Tintwistle. She remembered with fondness the day, centuries ago, when Godfrey, Anak and she had begun the project of the place of Man. The book had been written by Anak shortly before he died. The thousands of years that had since passed seemed like a few days.

Anak died three months after Albert and Edna ate from the Cancer Tree. So poisonous was its fruit, it had devastating consequences even as far as Tintwistle. In those days, the descendants of Anak were still in the land, though they were few.

Godfrey sat with his hands behind his head, looking at the clouds with a big smile on his face. Jack was cooking things on the barbecue he had built a few years before. Turning the meat now and then and waving smoke out of his eyes, Jack was happy.

' Dad, how many more times are you going to try and redeem those humans?'

As Godfrey replied, the smile left his face. 'You know the answer to that, Jack.'

Sophia stopped reading and stared into the distance where Philip was emptying the lawn cuttings into Eric's wheelbarrow.

'That Cancer Tree needs dealing with, Dad. Look at the history of this place. Albert and Edna start well, but are deceived by a boggart disguised as a rat. Then years go by with hardly anyone able to see or hear us. Then Norman seeks us out at a time when the boggarts tried to wipe humans out altogether. But he gets mental problems through being the only surviving family after the flood, and ends his days drunk and naked.'

'Jack, do we have to do this now? Can't we just

enjoy the sunshine?'

'Dad, I am just asking if it is still possible to keep making these deals with humans when their frailty breaks the agreement. Why do you go on and on forgiving, and trying again with someone else?'

'Well that's what your old Dad does, Jack. Sophia and I have called a new human, who we think will do really well.'

'Who have you found now?'

'Erm, Martin Simmonite is his name.'

'Disturbing name! You know there was a guy with that name, ages ago, who killed an Italian in Ancoats, and then ran away from the scene, and from his wife and children.'

Godfrey grinned, in embarrassment, and then looked at Jack and then away again.

'Dad! Don't tell me you are recruiting killers now!'
'Jack, the humans are made in our image but, since they were infected by the Cancer Tree, they are unable to be quite like us. But in order that they survive, I have to keep trying until the right time comes to deal with the Cancer Tree.'

'The right time?'

'Jack, can we talk about this some other time?'

Sophia stood and waved at Philip and Eric in the distance. A few other angels, who had been working in the greenhouses, saw Philip and Eric down tools and joined them.

Jack made sure they all had drinks, food, and a place to sit.

Godfrey poured a glass of red wine. He was pondering again and looking into the distance.

Sophia stood slightly apart from the little party and looked down the drive to the narrow gate as though she was expecting someone. A tear fell from her eye. She took a sip of her white wine then quietly began to sing. The angels folded their wings. They looked down the drive and then looked at each other.

o0o

Martin Simmonite was weary. He was weary from forty years on the run. He had moved around various farms near Daisy Nook doing seasonal work – harvesting crops, fruit picking, sheep shearing, and he had spent far too many days standing in a field in the Lancashire drizzle, feeding and milking cows. The summer months were easier as he worked on the travelling fair that came to Daisy Nook. After the fair left, he worked a few weeks at the little tea shop at Crime Lake. He didn't know why it was called Crime Lake, and that disturbed him. He always thought that any day now his crime would be exposed, and he would be jailed for the killing of the Italian in Ancoats.

As the years passed, he grew ever more weary and often wondered about his wife and children and what had become of them. As he became more and more dysfunctional he retreated into a secluded existence. He took to living by the River Medlock near Green Lane. He wept most afternoons.

One close, overcast day he went for a walk looking for shade and moving air. He found a little gravel lane that stretched into the trees on the hillside and decided to explore. He seemed to carry the weight of the man he had killed on his back.

Then he did something that several people had done

before him. He wandered into Bluebell Woods and began to have a thought he had never had before:

No matter how far you run ... you can never run away from yourself.

For Martin Simmonite that was quite a deep thought.

Simmonite

- ultimately derives from the Hebrew personal name 'Shimeon', meaning 'one who listens'

As he walked by a stream, he looked up at a hillside to see a rhododendron bush that was burning. He climbed the slope to get a better look. As he got near he realised it wasn't a bush on fire– there was a dazzling light just beyond it, by a narrow gate in a high wall. Martin shaded his eyes to look at the gate more closely and saw some faded lettering.

"Come in. All are welcome" he managed to make out. He turned the handle and the narrow gate opened.

o0o

The peacocks shrieked their usual welcome.

Godfrey handed his kebab back to Jack and set off running down the drive towards Martin Simmonite.

'He's come! He's come, Jack! His heart is still soft!'

Martin had always been disturbed by people running

towards him. He always assumed it was the Italians coming to get revenge. He stopped in his tracks, transfixed and shaking as he saw Godfrey approaching. He was tired of running away. He decided the Italians could have their revenge. He braced himself. He was ready to die.

But it wasn't the Italians. It was Godfrey in his green dungarees.

'Martin! My dear child!' he said, embracing him. 'I'm so glad you came. Not everyone we call comes to us. Come and rest a while with us. Eat. Drink. Be yourself.'

Martin was very quiet as he ate and drank. He thanked Philip and Eric for the generous offer of yet more angel cake, but politely declined. He wasn't a cake person.

As Jack and Godfrey welcomed him and showed him to an old oak lounger under a willow tree, Martin began to relax. He thought he'd died and gone to heaven, which in a way, he had.

'You need to rest, Martin. Why don't you stay the night?' asked Godfrey.

Martin had been on the run for too long to refuse. Jack showed him to a room with a lovely view of the park, and Martin collapsed on the large bed, fully dressed, and caught up on all the sleep he had missed for the last few decades.

'How are you doing, Mr Simmonite?' asked Jack.

'Huh?' said Martin, waking from a deep sleep.

'You've had twelve hours sleep young man. I thought you may be hungry.' said Jack

Martin hadn't felt young for a long time but, compared to Jack, perhaps he was. He sat up and Jack lit a small oil lamp but didn't open the curtains.

Jack placed a tray before Martin, who scratched his head and blinked his eyes.

'Coffee, bacon and eggs, toast and marmalade - I think I recall that is your favourite breakfast.' said Jack.

'How do you know that?' asked Martin, astonished by the perfect breakfast before him.

'I knew you before you were born, Lad.' said Jack.

'Wow! This is perfect.' said Martin.

'Now, the bathroom is here,' said Jack, opening the door to the en suite. 'It's a bit chilly tonight, so we are in the library with a log fire. When you are ready, wander down and we will have drinks and chats.'

Martin wolfed down the breakfast as though it was his last meal, and then bathed and showered at length. He had his first shave in a decade, and even found new clothes laid out for him. He felt like a new man, which he was.

Finally transformed, he went downstairs and looked for the library. At the end of the long hallway a door stood slightly open, and the glow of the log fire and the dulcet tones of conversation drew him towards the room. He was warmly welcomed by Godfrey, Jack and Sophia, who were drinking wine and eating nuts and nibbles by the log fire. The room was lined with walls of books on all four sides. In the big bay window, Martin noticed a large desk with small stacks of books and a notepad open, as though someone was in the middle of some research.

'Vin rouge?' asked Godfrey puffing on his pipe.

'Nuts?' asked Jack smiling.

'Thank you so much.' said Martin.

'Have a seat, Lad,' said Godfrey, pouring a glass of the red stuff.

Jack pushed the bowl of nuts towards Martin, as he tossed one in the air and caught it in his mouth.

'He shoots. He scores!' laughed Jack.

Sophia was slightly more subdued - gazing into the flames of the fire, and sipping a small white wine spritzer.

During the course of the evening, Martin broke down and confessed to the murder of the Italian all those decades before. Godfrey informed him that they knew all about it and that he had been in Ancoats that night and witnessed the whole scene.

'He was a very angry and violent man,' said Godfrey. 'He came here the night you killed him – as his last breath left him. He stayed in that room you slept in last night. He's changed for the better now.'

Martin had no idea what to make of this new information. He desperately wanted to ask where the man was now, but he couldn't force the question from his lips. He was overwhelmed by the incredible grace and mercy shown towards him. He felt so out of place sat by the fire with these three amazing people ... and yet, at the same time, he felt he had finally come home.

After more drinks and snacks, and various stories and anecdotes, Godfrey decided it was time for sleep. Although Martin had only woken up a few hours earlier, he was up for more sleep. The years he had spent running from himself had been exhausting. He returned to his room, but this time climbed under the sheets and rested properly.

After breakfast next morning, Jack went off with Philip and Eric to plan the day's gardening jobs and other angel activities. Godfrey invited Martin to walk with him in the garden towards the boundary wall on the far side of the park, past the tennis courts. As they chatted, Martin was disturbed by the sound of weeping. At first he didn't want to interrupt Godfrey, and he tried to ignore it. But it became too much.

'Godfrey, can't you hear that sound of weeping?'

'You can hear it then?'

'Yes of course! It is really distressing.'

'It is distressing. They are distressed people. I've been listening to that for many days.'

'Pardon me, but if you have heard that weeping for so long why have you not done something about it?'

'Oh, as soon as I heard it the first time, I did something about it.'

'Well what did you do? Because I don't think it is helping those people! Listen to them!'

'What I did was to call you to come here, Martin.'

'What?'

'The problem and the answer for these people is you,' Godfrey looked Martin in the eye. 'I made you to be a leader to these people. But since the day you fled that crime scene, they have had no leader. They became victims and ended up in poverty. Right now, all your descendants and your community are suffering badly. In fact, your own wife and children are crying tonight. The cries you can hear are your own people and your own family.'

Martin swallowed hard. The thought of his wife and

children crying like that was hard to take.

'Martin, your people fell into poverty after you ran away. Most of them ended up in the workhouse. They are being used as forced labour to make bricks at Newton Heath Brickworks. The conditions are terrible. I want you to go and set them free.'

'How can I do that? Who am I?'

'You are their leader and their saviour. I have made you to be that person.'

'What?! No!' said Martin. Being on the run for decades, he wasn't used to taking responsibility.

'Oh, it gets worse.'

'How could it possibly get worse?'

'Well, the Brickworks is run by the younger brother of the Italian you killed.'

'What?'

'Yes. And your wife and children are trapped there. This is your chance to redeem yourself. The cave you fear to enter holds the treasure you seek. Do this and you will find peace at last.'

Martin wanted to stick a big fat fist right in Godfrey's mouth. He wanted to stick his fingers in his ears and sing 'la-la-la-la-la' very loud, to drown out Godfrey's words. But he knew his time had come. He had let his family down but now he could redeem himself, and them, but only if Godfrey would help him. Part of him regretted ever coming through the narrow gate, but part of him felt he was finally going to resolve his inner conflict once and for all.

12

The Brickworks

Tucked away at Windsor Road, in Failsworth, the second largest mansion along the road belonged to an Italian immigrant named Antonio Acerbi. It was curious that several mansions had sprung up on Windsor Road. They all backed onto Bluebell Woods near the narrow gate and Jack's mansion at Brookdale. Yet none of the owners had ever found it. The narrow gate only seemed to be found by the poor, the desperate or people who were intentionally looking for it. Those who were self-assured, arrogant or indifferent could walk by that gate every day but never see it. Martin Simmonite had stumbled upon it. Antonio Acerbi had walked past it may times walking his dogs. He had never noticed it. His mind and heart were elsewhere.

He had made his millions by making bricks. As Manchester had grown rapidly, people had stopped building wooden houses and had started using bricks. Since the cotton mills had sprung up, the city needed millions of bricks every month. Forty years ago he was involved in a violent fight one night with some locals in

Ancoats. In the melee that ensued, Antonio discovered his older brother dead on the ground, bleeding from the ears. At the side of the road, near a crumbling wall, he had noticed a heap of bricks. He picked one up and began to threaten his opponents.

As he and his cousins carried his dead brother home that night, he believed they had escaped with their lives because of those bricks. After his brother's funeral he became obsessed with bricks. Soon he was working at a brickworks in Miles Platting, and before long he was a manager.

He borrowed a substantial amount of money from three uncles, and soon opened his own brickworks at Newton Heath. All was going well. He made his fortune. But then coal became expensive; feeding the hellish glow of the brick kilns required a constant cheap supply. Workers in Manchester began to rise up and demand higher pay.

There were still, however, a large number of the poor in workhouses, who would do anything for a daily meal and a pittance to survive. They had, out of necessity, applied to the workhouse and in turn been directed to Newton Heath Brickworks, where they worked in hellish conditions six days a week from 6am to 8pm. Children as young as five-years-old were expected to work daily in the sweltering heat. Many infants had died there.

Antonio Acerbi knew a business opportunity when he saw one - cheap labour and reduced costs. This arrangement was now fully financing his privileged lifestyle. His happiness now depended on the misery of the poor. Frankly, as long as the profits from brick production were coming in, he didn't really care about anyone else.

One morning, he was taking his breakfast on the back lawn, in the summer sunshine, when his butler brought the toast and the mail.

'Sir, there is a visitor who says he has a very important proposition to put to you.'

Antonio was distracted by the newspaper headlines that said coal prices were to increase again. Used to investors calling in for breakfast and conversations about new investment opportunities, Antonio waved to the butler, 'Yes, of course. Show him in.'

Looking across to Bluebell Woods, he heard a Green Woodpecker laugh. He took the silver lid off the butter dish and spread butter across his warm toast, then spooned on a thick layer of marmalade.

He took a sip of his freshly brewed coffee and bit into the toast. Life was good.

'Ahem.'

Antonio looked round to see his butler offering a chair at the table to a slightly dishevelled figure, who looked distinctly out of place in this grand scene.

'Thank you for agreeing to see me,' said Martin Simmonite, looking rather nervously at Antonio.

Antonio's mouth fell open and he put the newspaper down.

'I am sure my family and my community are extremely grateful to you for employing them when no one else would. You have graciously helped them through a dark time,' he continued. 'But now the time has come for change.'

Antonio dropped his toast and stared at Martin.

'I have had an encounter with Godfrey.'

Martin paused to see if the mention of Godfrey would impact the wall of disdain he was encountering. Antonio continued to look at him like he was sniffing something undesirable he had just found on the bottom of his shoe.

'Who the hell are you?' demanded Antonio.

'I am who I am,' said Martin, smiling nervously.

'What?' said Antonio, becoming increasingly irritated.

'I am the head of the family and community who are making your bricks at Briscoe Lane,' said Martin.

'Well why don't you shift your sorry backside off my chair, and get down there and make some friggin' bricks!' shouted Antonio.

'Well, Sir, No. I am here to tell you that Godfrey is calling my people to another district for a better life. They have served you well. But I am here to say that Godfrey says it's time to let my people go– to let them go and find new employment.' Martin was feeling increasingly uncomfortable.

Antonio swept his arm across the table sending all the breakfast things onto the lawn. He stood and leaned right in towards Martin's face.

'Your family are scum. You are scum. Without people like me supporting them and finding them things to do they'd all starve. You are a bunch of lazy parasites. You brought me a message did you? Well, messenger boy, get down to the Brickworks and tell your scummy relatives that if they don't double production by this time next week no one will get paid and the free lunch will not be provided!'

Antonio was referring to a cup of water and a small

chunk of bread that the workers were given fifteen minutes to eat. 'But Godfrey ...' began Martin.

'Who the hell is Godfrey? I am Antonio Acerbi! I am a key person in Manchester. You look like something the cat dragged in. Now get out!'

Martin was so intimidated by Antonio, not only because he was wealthy and angry, but also because he carried the secret that he had unintentionally killed Antonio's older brother. Perhaps Antonio's anger was rooted in that incident.

Martin stood up and left. The butler led him to the front door with respect but without a word being spoken.

For the best part of the next year, Martin began a campaign to free his people from the awful conditions at the brickworks. Unfortunately, his people had all become indentured slaves to Antonio.

Week after week, again and again, Martin brought the conditions in that place to public attention and to the attention of the leaders of the town. But every time Antonio was challenged he kept making things harder for the workers; increasing their hours without increasing their meagre pay and demanding more bricks to be made per hour. Finally, after Antonio became frustrated with being under constant and sustained pressure, he said they could leave.

Martin told his people to collect their few belongings and to meet outside the Brickworks within the hour. When they had gathered, he led them towards Clayton Vale and towards freedom.

The Brickworks ground to a halt, and Antonio regretted caving in to the pressure. His investors were demanding to know why production had stopped and he began ranting at his managers. Calling his henchmen together, they found makeshift weapons – pickaxe handles, clubs and heavy sticks, which they sharpened at one end, then they set off in pursuit of Martin and the fleeing slaves. Martin was expecting trouble and kept looking back. He saw the mob approaching and urged his people to move faster.

They reached a part of the River Medlock where it runs deep. There were no bridges for miles in either direction. Martin and the people were trapped. Antonio's mob were chasing after them, down Culcheth Lane. Martin was unsure what to do, when suddenly he heard Godfrey's voice beside him. 'Stretch out your hand over the Medlock.'

Martin did as Godfrey said, and the waters began to separate and stand up in a wall on the right and on the left. Seeing a path across the riverbed, the people ran across as fast as they could. As the last one reached the other side, Martin saw the mob coming down the hillside. They began to follow them across the dry riverbed when Martin lowered his hand. The River Medlock began to flow fiercely again and the Italians were washed down river. Some of them drowned. Martin and his people were free at last.

They walked as far as Denton that day and camped there for the night. Day after day he kept his people moving and found himself and his place among them. A deeper peace grew in him, as he took up his role of husband and father once more. Obviously the betrayal his wife, Zoe, felt was deep. The regret he felt for leaving her for forty years with no explanation was like a black hole in his soul. Their relationship was at best dysfunctional. But there were a few moments of laughter and love. Nothing could make up for forty years of separation, but at least now Martin had delivered their whole family from the clutches of Antonio.

They journeyed on through Marple and Whaley Bridge, into the High Peaks of Derbyshire. And there they lived for many years, in a deserted wilderness. Some of them began to breed sheep and goats, and became herdsmen. Others became coal miners and sold coal to nearby towns.

As the community settled down to freedom, their human frailty was revealed. People began lying to each other and cheating. Disputes broke out and Martin often had to settle arguments between families. In the darkest times the people even killed each other. Martin was wearied; he just wanted the people to live peacefully with one another.

One day, he told the people that they needed to meet Godfrey, and then they would understand what life was really about. He led the people across the hills towards Godfrey's tower. But as the people drew near to Hartshead Pike, the sky turned dark and foreboding. Soon a storm blew up and thunder rumbled all around them. Lightning flashes revealed Godfrey's tower silhouetted against the sky. The people became fearful. There was something very holy on that hill and the people felt they would be destroyed if they stepped through the narrow gate.

'You and your brother Arthur go up and speak to Godfrey,' the people told Martin. 'Then come and tell us what he said. We will do whatever Godfrey says, but do not make us go through the narrow gate or we will die.'

Once the two brothers stepped through the narrow gate, the sky didn't appear half as stormy as it did from the bottom of the hill.

Arthur walked a few steps behind Martin, as it was his first time to meet Godfrey. He wasn't sure what to expect and wondered if the people had been right. His fears were soon put to rest when Godfrey came out to greet them.

'Martin! Great to see you again. And you must be Arthur!'

Godfrey gave them both a hug.

'Come in and we'll get the kettle on.'

Arthur looked around the tower and saw Godfrey's books on the first-floor balcony.

As the three of them talked, Martin and Arthur noticed a large object standing against the wall, draped in a golden cloth.

Godfrey noticed their attention was distracted.

'Well I guess it is time!' he said.

'Time for what?' asked Martin.

'I have been thinking about your community problems for some time. I was chatting to Jack and Sophia about it and we have made you a gift. We think it will help.'

Godfrey pulled the golden cloth off the large object to reveal a rosewood upright piano. 'The timber parts were made by Jack. The strings and other parts were made by Sophia. I tuned it myself. And the most important part– I engraved with my own hands.'

Next to the brass candleholders, on the front panel of the piano, Godfrey had fixed two slate plaques. They read:

Ten tips for physical, mental and spiritual health:

1. I am Godfrey, who rescued your ancestors from slavery in the brickworks. Keep connected to me, and life will flow into you.

2. Don't make statues of animals and stuff, and then start worshipping them. They don't possess the ability to love like I do. Worshipping statues will draw you towards boggarts, and their deathly touch will bring sadness to your life.

3. Please don't tell people that I told you something, when it is really just your personal idea, opinion or even stupidity. If I really do tell you something, you'll never have to prefix your statement with 'Godfrey told me ...' My words carry their own power. Do not misuse my name.

4. Humans' power supply needs charging fully every seven days. So every seven days recharge yourself by having a complete day of rest.

5. Honour your Mum and Dad. They may disturb you from time to time but they gave you life. They cared for you when you were helpless. They didn't have an instruction book so maybe they made mistakes. Don't get bitter with them. Love them. It will go much better for you if you honour them.

6. Never let hate take such a hold on you that you murder someone. Look around you. Everything I made strives for life. Death is what boggarts love. Don't be a boggart. Be a human. Forgive one another.

7. Love your spouse. You committed yourselves to each other. Cheating on your spouse will cause great pain to your spouse, your children and your friends. And for you, it will cause a deep hurt and regret in your heart that you will carry for a very long time.

8. Don't steal things. You wouldn't like it if someone stole your things. So don't do that to others.

9. Don't tell lies about people. You don't like it when they do it to you, so don't do it to them.

10. Don't desire everything your friends and neighbours have. When you desire something, ask yourself why you need it. Will it fulfil a real purpose, or are you just trying to be like everyone else?

Martin and Arthur didn't know what to say.

Godfrey sat down and began to play the piano. He sang the song of creation and a cloud of peacefulness enveloped the whole of the tower. Martin and Arthur had never felt such a deep peace before.

Soon Martin found himself sitting at the piano and playing it perfectly, though how that was happening he was not sure.

Godfrey told the brothers to take the piano and keep it in the community. In any time of trouble they should gather the people and Martin should play the piano. Peace would come to the community.

'If ever you are under attack from enemies, bring out the piano and my protection will be with you,' said

Godfrey. 'And teach the people about my ten tips for a healthy and peaceful life.'

Soon Godfrey was helping Martin and Arthur lift the piano down the front steps of the tower. He went back in and fetched a little piano-moving trolley. They lifted the piano onto the trolley and Godfrey helped them wheel it down to the narrow gate. They said their goodbyes and Godfrey returned to his tower.

The people were wondering what was taking Martin and Arthur so long, when through the swirling mist they saw two figures emerge, pushing a piano.

Martin called for Billy Briggs to bring his horse and cart. Soon Martin and Arthur had lifted the piano onto Billy's cart, and then Martin read out the ten tips for good health. After that, Martin sat at the piano and played the tunes that Godfrey had taught him. Just as Godfrey had said, a great peace descended on the people.

13

The Lighthouse

Down below, on the beach, many families from Manchester were enjoying their annual holiday in North Wales. Dads were helping children build sandcastles. Mums were unpacking picnics made that morning. Children were paddling in the sea. The sky and the sea were blue and a gentle breeze took the edge off the soaring temperature.

People were so busy enjoying their holiday that no one noticed Salty Tom had a guest. Godfrey loved to spend his annual holiday with Tom in Talacre lighthouse. From the balcony, Godfrey could enjoy the views out to sea that Tom enjoyed every day. And for miles inland too, the views were inspiring.

Perhaps it seems odd that Godfrey lived in a tower on a hill near Oldham but also liked to holiday in a tower - the lighthouse at Talacre. But Godfrey always preferred to see the bigger view. Stepping back from things had always enabled him to see what others could not see. He reckoned that most conflicts were caused by people not stepping back to see the bigger picture.

Tom had been a good friend to Godfrey for years. Although Tom was a mere mortal, Godfrey felt he had a lot of wisdom. His many hours alone at the lighthouse gave him a lot of time to ponder. And like Godfrey, Tom enjoyed a good ponder.

Godfrey had been telling Tom about Martin Simmonite, and how he had led his people out of slavery from the brickworks.

'The thing is, Tom, I wanted them to be free from slavery, but it was not my intention that they should live on the hills in the wilderness, slaves to the elements. I was hoping Martin would have led them back to Manchester by now. That is the land I promised their ancestors.'

Tom tapped his pipe on the balcony railings and the ash blew away in the breeze. He refilled it and lit it again, taking a few puffs of his pipe as he let his gaze rest on the horizon.

'He'll never go back there, Boyo,' said Tom. 'Manchester is everything he is afraid of.'

'I suppose,' said Godfrey as he sipped a small glass of cold beer.

'He probably can't believe he came face to face with the brother of the man he killed and survived,' said Tom. 'He'll not risk it a second time. Does he have a younger man who could be his successor?'

'He does - someone by the name of Steven Bailey,' said Godfrey. 'Yes. Perhaps he is the one who will bring the people back to Manchester.'

'I think most of us humans only have one big thing in us, Boyo. You know – one thing we really give our life to. A few seem to do two big things. But most of us can only manage one big thing. As Mr Simmonite has carried the guilt of a murder all his life, he did well to get his people out of slavery,' said Tom.

'You know, Tom, I always have higher hopes for you humans than you seem to realise. I thought he would lead them out of slavery and then be the obvious person to lead them home,' said Godfrey.

'Ah, if the Cancer Tree hadn't crippled us humans, I am sure we would all be doing better. That's the real problem. We are all a bit dysfunctional, just as the boggarts planned we would be,' said Tom.

'Yes. Them there boggarts did strike a huge blow against life and light with that,' said Godfrey frowning.

'You're Godfrey! Can't you sort that out, Boyo?'

'Ahhh ... Let's not go there, Tom.'

'The cave you fear to enter holds the treasure you seek. Isn't that what you told Martin Simmonite all those years ago?' asked Tom.

'That is true. I did say that. And for you humans it is almost always true,' said Godfrey. 'And no doubt it is true for me. But the cost ...' Godfrey took another swig of beer.

'What would it cost you? Curing the effects of the Cancer Tree would be huge. What do you have that you are unwilling to sacrifice for the freedom of humans from the Cancer Tree?' asked Tom.

'It's not 'what' it is 'who',' said Godfrey.

'Sorry, Boyo? I don't understand,' said Tom.

'There is only one person who can overthrow the effects of the Cancer Tree, Tom. Our Jack is the only one able to do that. But it would mean letting him go and losing him. I can't begin to imagine losing my only son, Tom,' said Godfrey.

'Right you are, Boyo. If that is the price of our freedom, then I understand. To lose a son is far too high a price. I see now,' said Tom, puffing on his pipe. 'I see why you are exploring all other options.'

'There aren't any other options really, Tom,' said Godfrey. 'But I love you humans so much. I have no choice but to rescue you, boggarts or no boggarts. And Jack, well, Jack is the apple of my eye. The thought of losing him ...'

Tom didn't reply. He was beginning to feel awkward that he had pushed his special friend to discuss something so personal and difficult.

'Tom, don't feel bad. You have helped me think this through. I really need to explain to Jack what is involved and then let him make the decision. I have just always felt that would be an impossible burden to put on my boy.'

As the pair talked further, the clear blue sky began to dim and the evening painted red streaks across the heavens. The two friends sat silently for a few moments, looking out to sea.

'Right, Boyo,' said Tom, 'time to put the big light on.'

Tom went inside and flicked a couple of switches and then pulled a big lever. There was a deep whirring sound and the massive reflectors in the tower began to turn. He pulled another lever and an incredible bright light burst into life. The beam was visible out at sea, even though full darkness had not yet fallen.

Tom popped his head out of the window. 'I'm nipping out to get some fish and chips, Godfrey! I'll leave you to keep a look out ... for those in peril on the sea.'

Down below, families were collecting their belongings and leaving the beach for their holiday dwellings. A cold breeze began to blow. Godfrey looked over the rail and watched the tiny figure of Tom making his way to the local chip shop.

Godfrey sat back in his chair and pondered. As he watched the beam of light from the lighthouse scan the horizon out to sea, a tear fell from his eye.

'The light shines in the darkness, and the darkness has not overcome it,' whispered Godfrey to himself.

Twenty minutes later he saw Tom walking back across the sands with a package wrapped in newspaper under his arm.

'Time to put the kettle on, butter some bread and warm the plates,' said Godfrey, going down the spiral stairs to Tom's kitchen.

14

Red Lights and Red Rope

It was overcast with a constant drizzle the day Martin Simmonite was buried. He had lived to be one-hundred-and-twenty-years-old, and never looked his age. All the families and their descendants who Martin Simmonite had led from slavery at Newton Heath brickworks were there that day. He was buried on a hilltop near Edale, in a grave marked only by a stack of stones. As the drizzle soaked the assembled crowd, Steven Bailey conducted the ceremony. He spoke with fondness of his old friend. For sure, Martin had been like a father to Steven Bailey.

Before he died, Martin Simmonite had laid his hands on Steven Bailey and blessed him. He had given him instructions to lead the people into their promised land in Manchester. He had taught him how to hear the voice of Godfrey to direct and guide him.

Perhaps the most important thing Martin had done was to bequeath his sacred piano. Martin's piano had been a gift from Godfrey.

On this particular rainy day, everyone that had

gathered understood this was the end of an era. They liked Steven Bailey but they had always seen him as Martin's sidekick, not their main leader. However, they appreciated the dignity and humility of Steven Bailey as he honoured Martin's memory that day. At Steven's signal the gravediggers began to fill in the grave with soil. Sadness and the Northern drizzle rested on the people for the next thirty days.

One weekend, before Martin's death, Steven had walked with him as far as Tintwistle and they had camped out in the ruins of Anak's Castle. Martin gave many instructions to Steven, who hadn't entirely taken in all the information, as he had assumed that Martin would lead the move into the promised land.

Bereft of his closest friend, and a little depressed, Steven went on a long walk one weekend, alone. He was sitting in a small wood, eating a snack he had packed for himself, when he thought he heard singing in the distance. It was a haunting song that reminded him of sacred moments when Martin had played the piano, and a holy quietness had fallen on the people.

He stood to see if he could detect which direction it was coming from. He walked further and then came to the edge of the woods. He looked out across a field over to a hill in the distance. Yes. The song was coming from there. He began to walk towards the sound of singing.

Before long he saw an old tower on a hill in the distance. He wiped the raindrops from his face to get a better look. Yes. The song was coming from the tower. He set off towards it at a renewed pace. Who could sing like that? Was Martin still alive? What did all this mean? So many questions ran through his mind. As he reached the foot of the hill he was breathing heavily, having almost ran the last mile. He passed through a narrow gate at the boundary of the hill and set off for the summit. As he did, he noticed the rain had stopped and blue sky was appearing. He paused for breath for a moment, as the hill was steep, and looked towards the tower.

The singing stopped and a sacred silence hung in the air. And then, as Steven Bailey looked towards the tower, he saw a strange figure running towards him. It wasn't a human, an angel or a boggart. It was something he had never seen before. Green dungarees, curly black hair and laughter. Yes, the person running towards him was laughing. As he approached, a realisation swept over him – it was Godfrey. His jaw dropped open.

'Steven Bailey! You came! Well done!' Godfrey embraced the startled visitor.

Steven Bailey had not been hugged like that ... well, ever. His mourning for Martin seemed to drain out of him and was washed away all in a moment. He shook. He cried a little. He laughed. He shook his head in disbelief.

'Come! Come my dear, dear friend,' said Godfrey, pointing to the tower. He took Steven's backpack and walked with him up the hill.

'Wonderful! Fantastic! Ha ha!' chuckled Godfrey.

They reached the tower at Hartshead Pike and Godfrey showed Steven to a chair.

'Sit down, Lad. A brew? No! We'll need something better than that.'

Steven looked around the tower. He looked up to the first floor balcony and all the books lining the tower.

Godfrey came out of the back kitchen with two wine glasses and a nice bottle of red wine.

'Vin rouge, Steven?'

'Well, if you are having one ...'

Godfrey poured two good glasses of red wine, and sat in the other chair near Steven.

'Martin is dead,' said Godfrey, looking Steven directly in the eye.

'Erm ... yes I know that,' said Steven looking confused.

'I don't think you do, young Steven.' said Godfrey.

'With respect Sir, I conducted his funeral,' assured Steven.

'Yes I know that,' said Godfrey, 'but you are living as though he is coming back. He isn't.'

Steven looked at Godfrey with a realisation stirring in his heart.

'Martin is dead, Steven. So now you – Steven Bailey – must arise. Your apprenticeship is over. You must rise up and lead these people into the land I promised them.'

Steven swallowed hard.

'Be strong, Steven. Be strong and courageous. Every place that the sole of your foot treads I will give you, as I said to Martin. From Stockport in the South to Rochdale in the North, from Urmston in the West to Droylsden in the East– all shall be your territory. No man shall be able to stand before you all the days of your life. As I was with Martin, so I will be with you. I will never leave you or forsake you.'

Steven Bailey was shaking so much that his red wine was spilling over the edge of his glass. He took a large swig.

'Be strong and courageous, Steven.'

Eventually, Steven grasped what it was like to meet Godfrey. He calmed down a bit and asked a few questions. Godfrey liked people who asked questions. It showed that they were seeking the truth.

Godfrey had a Lancashire hotpot in the oven, and soon the smell of lamb and vegetables drifted into the front room.

'Time for tea!' said Godfrey.

He motioned for Steven to come and sit at the table in the corner of the room. Soon the wonderful hotpot was served, and more wine, and a stack of bread and butter.

Steven forgot about his daily duties as leader, for a while, and just became Steven again. For a few moments that night he wasn't a son, or a brother, or a father, or a husband, or a grandfather. Steven was just Steven. And being just Steven for a few hours helped him to find himself; it helped him step into his new role as leader.

oOo

The smell of bacon butties and fresh coffee was still in the air the next morning as Steven Bailey said farewell to Godfrey and set off back to his people. He had slept so well in Godfrey's guest room. The sky was blue, and the warm breeze that blew from behind him seemed to urge him back to his task. As he got to the narrow gate at the foot of the hill, he turned and waved to Godfrey. Godfrey, puffing on his pipe, waved back and chuckled to himself.

On his return to the camp at Edale, Steven gathered

the heads of all the clans and told them of the move to Manchester. Within three days the people were on the move again. This time, the special cart built to carry Martin's piano led the way. Four horses pulled the cart and the wooden wheels bumped over the ground. Although the piano was tied down, two men sat on the cart to keep it from falling. They journeyed to a deserted place and camped for the night. Today this place is called 'Hyde' because Steven Bailey's people hid there before taking the land.

Back then, Manchester and the surrounding areas were dark, brutal places. The light of Godfrey was almost lost there. The Irish and the Italians, who had come to dwell there, fought street battles most nights. The original occupants had followed the ways of the boggarts, and were sacrificing children in fires to please them. Death always pleased the boggarts.

Many women had fallen into prostitution because the love of many had grown cold. Love was rare but every man lusted after women.

The people camped in Hyde for three nights and prepared themselves. Steven Bailey called two young men to him. He gave them instructions to spy on the land of Stockport.

'Now, boys, get a good look around and find out all you can. Forewarned is forearmed.'

Joe and Henry were excited at being given the mission and set off at sunset. They were used to mundane jobs, looking after sheep, and camping out on the hills. Joe could hardly contain himself.

'This is fantastic!'

'I know,' said Henry. 'Steven Bailey chose us nobodies!'

'No. No, I mean this is fantastic. We could be getting sex tonight!'

'What?'

'Henry! Wake up! Stockport? Haven't you heard that it is full of women who'll do anything you want for a few bob?'

'I thought we were on a mission to spy on the land,'

'Yes. Of course. But why don't we spy out a couple of ladies first, and then we'll go on a walk about? It's a win-win situation.'

'I suppose we could ...' said Henry.

Stockport Castle had a high, impenetrable outer wall. There was no way two shepherd boys could get through that. They reached the road near Bredbury, and found a convoy of carts taking wool to Stockport. If one of the wagon drivers was willing to let them ride for a skin of wine, they could hide deep in the wool and get past the gate. Sure enough they found a willing accomplice.

As Joe and Henry felt the cart roll onto cobbled streets, and heard music and shouting from the town, they knew their plan had worked.

'We're in!' whispered Joe.

Their driver, the worse for drink, turned a corner too tightly and drove his cart into a wooden building. The damage was significant and the owner of the house came out and an argument ensued.

'Run!' said Joe, jumping off the wagon.

'Flippin' 'eck!' said Henry, following his friend.

Soon the pair were just a couple of peasants, walking down a side street like any other two young men. They stumbled upon a busy market square, and several soldiers of the Mayor of Stockport were there on security duty. Joe and Henry slipped down a dark alley out of sight.

'Hello boys. Looking for a good time?' said a voice behind them.

Joe's mouth dropped open. Henry drooled.

Ingrid maintained eye contact with them both. 'See anything you like?'

They looked at her long dark hair, her dark eyes, and her glistening lips. Her black blouse was unbuttoned lower than they had ever seen, and also a bit see-through so that they could see her underwear... or lack of it.

Henry looked down to see a skirt much shorter than he had ever seen in all of his life on the Mountains of Ninepence.

'Oh – my – giddy – aunt ...' said Henry.

Joe observed Ingrid's legs and scanned her upwards, as Henry scanned her downwards.

'Come in boys,' said Ingrid, leading them through an open door, into a dimly lit room. 'Sit down. Relax.'

Relax was the last thing they could do. She poured them both a large glass of wine.

'Enjoy,' she said as she sat opposite them and crossed her legs in a way that made Henry spill some of his wine. Joe reached over and straightened Henry's wine glass.

'So how are you miss ...?' asked Joe.

'Ingrid. The name is Ingrid,' she said, leaning forwards.

Henry gazed down at her cleavage and began to spill his wine again. Joe elbowed him discretely in the ribs, and straightened his glass again.

'Now, how does this work, Ingrid?' asked Joe, trying to act more confident than he was.

'Well that's a good question.' She stood up and slowly turned around. 'First you check out the goods.'

Henry dropped his glass of wine, and hoped that no one noticed. Joe scowled at him.

'Stand up,' Ingrid said to Joe. Even her eye contact was giving Joe an experience he had never had before. She came close to him and embraced him. She looked him in the eye and then kissed him passionately. His knee trembled.

Henry was shaking so much he was trying to stop his chair making a noise.

Ingrid looked into Joe's eyes.

'You're not a Stockport boy are you?'

'Well, yes! Certainly. I mean ...'

'Hill people. That's what you two are.'

'No! No. My dear, we are Stockport born and bred!'

'Really? And yet still virgins?'

'No. Well. You see... Hang on.'

Henry was sitting with his mouth open and drooling, his eyes like saucers.

Suddenly, there was a bang on the door. The Mayor of Stockport's henchmen were doing a door-to-door search.

'Quick! Go up into the loft!' whispered Ingrid.

She pulled down the ladder and urged her visitors to hurry. Soon they were up in the darkness and Ingrid pushed up the ladder again. She straightened her hair and went to the front door.

'Oh Captain. Sorry. You caught me sleeping,' she

said, opening the door to the security men.

'It's 'Sergeant' actually,' said the officer. 'Now, we know a couple of the hill people got into town tonight and are spying on the land for an attempted invasion. We have reason to believe they are here.'

'Yes, Sergeant. They were here about an hour ago. Bloomin' cheek! But I sent them packing and they left the city going out towards Marple.'

The Sergeant had good reason not to cause Ingrid any trouble, as he had availed himself of Ingrid's charms on several occasions. Several occasions he had no desire for his wife to find out about, which is why Ingrid had pretended not to know he wasn't a Captain.

'Right,' he said, blushing slightly. 'Well thank you Madam for your help.'

'Oh it's Miss actually,' said Ingrid winking.

'Right men! Let's get after them!' urged the Sergeant, forcing an embarrassed smile in Ingrid's direction.

After the soldiers had gone, Ingrid pulled down the loft ladder and climbed up.

She called Joe and Henry to her. 'I know that Godfrey has given you this land. All the inhabitants of Stockport are faint-hearted because of your people. We have heard how Godfrey dried up the waters of the Medlock for you when you came out of Newton Heath. As soon as we heard these things, everyone was terrified.

Now, I'm asking you, since I have shown you kindness, that you'll also show kindness in return - to my family, and spare us and all that we have, and deliver our lives from death.'

Joe answered, 'We will, if you do not tell anything that happened here tonight. When Godfrey has given us the land, we will deal kindly towards you.'

She let them down by a rope through the window, as her house was built into the city wall.

Then Joe called up to Ingrid, 'Make sure you leave this red rope tied in your window. If you do not tie the red rope in your window, or you tell anyone what happened tonight, we will be released from our promise. The red rope will tell our people not to attack your house.'

'I understand! Get back safely!' called Ingrid. When they reached the ground she pulled the red rope back up but then let a small length out of the window and tied it there as her insurance in the coming battle.

'Bugger!' said Henry.

'What?' said Joe.

'One minute I'm about to lose my virginity to a stunning female, the next I am on the run and spending another night sleeping under a hedge with you!' said Henry.

'Yeah. Sorry about that Mate. I tried,' said Joe.

They crawled through the undergrowth for half a mile so as not to be spotted by the guards in the tower. Then they walked for miles in the dark. They found a dry hedge and settled down for the night.

'Sleep well, Henry,' said Joe.

'Whatever ...' said Henry.

15

Brass band

Steven Bailey was familiar with invasions and battles. Such occurrences were common in those days. Mayors, kings and local chiefs could be overthrown in a day. He knew how to plan a good war.

He was arranging his swordsmen, archers and fighters, and giving them a pep talk ready for the invasion the following morning. Everyone was prepared.

Early next morning they were ready to leave their camp in the grove of Acacia trees at Hyde. Forty-thousand nomads began their journey towards a more settled life. By nightfall, they saw Stockport Castle on the horizon. The people set up camp in a field. As was his daily discipline, Steven went for a walk at sunset. He walked towards the castle and stared at his objective. As he got nearer, he came across a small brook and skipped across. Looking up towards the castle, he saw a mighty warrior standing before him. The man was covered in armour and his sword was drawn. He looked Steven in the eye.

Steven remembered Godfrey's words – 'Be strong and very courageous.' He felt he had a supernatural authority in that moment and walked towards the powerful figure to challenge him.

'Are you for us or for our enemies?' he asked.

'No,' said the man.

'That doesn't even make sense!' said Steven. 'You have to be on our side or their side.'

'I come,' said the man, who seemed to glow, 'as the commander of this army.'

Steven was irritated, but only for a split second, as a revelation dawned on him. That night in Godfrey's tower, after Martin's funeral, Godfrey had told him to be strong and courageous. But he had also told him not to be surprised if Jack or Sophia appeared as he led the people into Manchester. His eyes were suddenly opened. He saw Jack stood in front of him. He saw him not only with his eyes but also with his heart.

'I see you,' he said, as he took off his sandals and knelt before the blazing light emanating from Jack.

'Steven, this is a special moment in the life of your people,' began Jack. 'It shall not be with weapons that you take Stockport, but with a brass band and a piano.'

Had it not been Jack saying this, Steven would have laughed. But there was an authority in Jack's words that rang true.

'How will that work?' asked Steven.

'Put your people in this order: Martin's piano shall lead the way, with your soldiers in front of it. Get the brass band to march behind it. Then the people.'

Steven scratched his head.

Jack continued as though all this sounded normal.

'For the next six days, march round the castle in silence. March round it once and then come back here.'

Steven gave him a quizzical look. He failed to understand this military strategy.

'Then on the seventh day you shall march around Stockport Castle seven times, with the brass band playing. When the trumpeters do their big finish, the walls of Stockport Castle will fall down.'

Steven got up from the ground and slapped himself across the face really hard. Then he bit his finger. No. He wasn't dreaming. Jack was actually stood in front of him and had given him those strange instructions. As he continued to look, Jack seemed to fade away. But Steven wondered if it was only his disbelief that made Jack disappear.

After a disturbed night's sleep, Steven Bailey finally made his peace with Jack's plan. He gathered the troops and briefed them of the plan. A few screwed their noses up and scratched their heads, but there was something like electricity in the air, and everyone felt this was the sort of thing that Martin Simmonite would have done if he was still alive.

And so the soldiers led Martin's piano, followed by the brass band and the people, and did as Steven Bailey had directed. Six days they marched around Stockport Castle in silence, and on the seventh day the brass band struck up some tunes. Steven began to play Martin's piano, as it was pulled along on the cart. On the seventh time round, the band did the 'big finish' with the trumpets ... and the ground began to shake. Masonry began to fall from the top of the castle walls. The people stepped back a short way and watched with open mouths as the huge castle began to crumble.

'Now!' shouted Steven.

The soldiers and the people ran into the city and it was taken easily. The promise to Ingrid and her family was kept; they survived the strange attack. Steven never did get to the bottom of why Ingrid had to be spared, but the two spies convinced him it was a matter of 'honour'.

That day, Steven became even more respected among the people. They began to build houses in the ruins there, and settled in the land.

The troops then invaded Levenshulme and then went on to Longsight. Steven swelled with pride but when the troops approached Ardwick they were defeated for the first time. This sent shock waves through the community.

Steven realised he had come to depend on his own strength and wisdom and had not listened for the voice of Jack.

The battle at Ancoats didn't go too well either, and Steven and his people fled across Angel Meadow and took Cheetham Hill. There, for many years, the people settled down and rested from war. They prospered in that place. Many became tailors and bakers.

The more they prospered, the more they moved further away from the centre of Manchester. They found pleasant places further out of town, near the countryside. There they continued to grow and settle as a community.

16

Big Gordon

One extremely hot summer day, many years after the days of Steven Bailey, Godfrey sat on the front step of his tower at Hartshead Pike. He observed a young lad herding sheep on the hills in the distance. As the sheep chewed their way across the grassy slopes, he noticed the lad walking towards the tower. The boy found the narrow gate at the bottom of the hill and Godfrey watched him as he approached.

'Excuse me Sir,' said the young man, 'sorry to trouble you, but do you have a cup of water? I am very thirsty.'

'It is no trouble, Douglas. No trouble at all. If anyone is thirsty, they can come to me and I'll give them a drink.'

'How do you know my name?'

'Ah, I know all about you, young man. How about a big glass of lemonade with a splash of lime cordial?'

'That would be wonderful.'

Godfrey went into the kitchen and came back with

two large glasses and a big jug of lemonade with a splash of lime cordial and ice cubes floating in it.

'Sit down, Lad.' Godfrey nodded towards the front step and then poured the thirst-quenching liquid into the two glasses and handed one to Douglas.

Godfrey asked Douglas a few questions and explained who he was, though Douglas had already realised he may have stumbled upon the legendary Godfrey.

'I don't really like minding my Dad's sheep,' said Douglas, looking across the hillside to check he still had them all in view.

'I know,' said Godfrey. 'But do it as well as you can to honour your Dad. It won't be forever.'

'Oh I think it may be,' said Douglas, shaking his head. 'I'm the youngest, you see. My older brothers are all in the army in Manchester. I'd love to be a soldier, instead of sitting on damp grass on these hills with those stupid sheep.'

'And what about that ukulele hung over your shoulder?' asked Godfrey.

'Oh that? That helps the boredom of watching sheep for hours on end. I write songs and stuff,' said Douglas. 'Do you want to hear one?'

'I'd love to,' said Godfrey smiling.

Douglas put down his drink on the step and took hold of his ukulele and began to strum and smile as he sang a few of his songs.

Godfrey beamed at the brilliance of the young lad.

'Aye. You'll not be looking after sheep for many more years Douglas. You have a gift there for sure!'

'Ah thank you Sir,' said Douglas, downing the rest

of his cold drink. He rolled the ice-cold glass across his forehead.

The two of them sat for a while enjoying the sunshine and each other's company.

'Wolf!' said Douglas suddenly. 'There's a flippin' wolf over there! Thanks for the drink Godfrey!'

He ran off down the hill towards the sheep, ukulele over his shoulder, and pulled a catapult out of his pocket.

'Bloody wolf! You're not having any of our Dad's sheep!' he yelled.

The wolf looked at Douglas and then back towards a young lamb with a limp. Douglas could see the wolf was prowling towards the herd, seeking one of them to devour. He leapt through the narrow gate and ran towards the wolf. The wolf decided to make its move and ran towards the limping lamb. Douglas took a pebble from his pocket and loaded the catapult. He took position and aimed. Seconds later, the wolf let out a howl as the pebble hit it between the eyes.

'Gotcha!' said Douglas, reloading his catapult. The wolf twitched on the ground before becoming very still. He approached the corpse – which by now was literally a 'bloody wolf' – and checked it was dead, before guiding the herd onwards across the hill.

That evening, when the sheep were all settled for the night, Douglas sat under a tree and had an idea for a new tune. He began to play his ukulele and sing of his strange meeting with Godfrey.

'O Godfrey, you are a true friend,
I shall seek you again;
My soul thirsts for you,
I long to meet you again, in a dry and weary land

where there is no water.
I have seen you in your tower and looked on your power.
Because your friendship is better than life, my lips will sing of you.'

He felt something change that day. The words of Godfrey had touched his heart. He began to believe that his days of being a shepherd boy would come to an end. Yes. There was more to his life than sheep.

oOo

Back when Stewart Ogden was the Mayor of Manchester, the city suffered a series of attacks from tribes from the East, in Yorkshire. But one day, a tribe from the West arrived near Manchester and began to cause trouble for the inhabitants.

Stewart Ogden summoned the troops and sent them to protect the city. When they reached a valley near Warrington, they saw the invaders lined up on a hillside. Giants no longer existed. The descendants of Anak had all died long ago. However, the invaders that day presented Big Gordon. He was the nearest thing to a giant the people had ever seen – standing at over eight feet tall. His bronze armour and spear glinted in the sunshine.

The invaders began to taunt the armies of Manchester. Big Gordon kept shouting 'Come and have a go if you think you're hard enough!' And every time he shouted it, fear took hold of the Manchester soldiers. For a whole week the stand-off developed, with neither side making any progress.

Back on the hills, on the other side of Manchester, Douglas sat by a stream keeping an eye on his Dad's sheep. He strummed on his ukulele as he worked on another new tune. At midday his father arrived to take over.

'Now son, I've packed some supplies for your brothers, with the army at Warrington. I want you to take the horse and cart and get over there by the end of the day.'

Douglas walked home with his ukulele over his shoulder. When he got home he found the supplies packed ready as his Dad had told him. He loaded the cart and set off for Warrington and the front line.

By sunset, Douglas arrived at the stand-off with Big Gordon. Both sides started to settle down for the night. Douglas found his older brothers but they were not pleased to see him.

'What are you doing here? Come to poke your nose in, have you?' said his eldest brother.

'What have I done wrong now?' asked Douglas. 'Dad sent me to bring you some supplies'

'Oh,' said his brother with a scowl, as he accepted the supplies.

Douglas wandered down the front line as his brothers unpacked the food and drink. He listened to various conversations and looked across the valley, towards the enemy lines. After dark, he went back to where he had tied his horse and cart, and slept under the cart for the night.

As morning gilded the sky, Douglas woke to the sound of the enemy banging their shields with their swords. Big Gordon was taunting the troops.

Douglas crawled out from under the cart and went to have a look. The day began to unfold as all the other days of the stand-off had, with no one willing to take on Big Gordon.

At midday Stewart Ogden arrived from Manchester to view the situation for himself. He too was afraid of Big Gordon. 'He is so big! How can we beat him?' everyone was asking.

But he was so enormous, that Douglas wondered how he could possibly miss.

He went to speak to one of Stewart's men and told them he was willing to fight Big Gordon.

'Yeah right!' the man said laughing.

'No. I am serious!' said Douglas. 'When I look after my Dad's sheep I have to defend them from wolves and foxes. A good size stone in my catapult sorts them out. I'll do the same to Big Gordon.'

The man looked at the boy and stroked his chin.

'You are being serious aren't you, young man?'

'Aye I am,' said Douglas.

The advisor went to see Stewart and told him of Douglas' offer.

'We don't have any armour that small!' said Stewart, looking at Douglas.

'I don't need armour! When I kill wolves and foxes, I don't have armour. Godfrey looks after me,' said Douglas.

Stewart was disturbed as the taunts of Big Gordon started again. He looked at Douglas.

'Alright, young man. I'm going to give you a chance,' said the Mayor.

Douglas was allowed through the front line, and all eyes watched as he walked towards Big Gordon. He stooped down several times to pick up several good size stones to put in his pocket.

As he approached the enemy, Big Gordon stepped forward.

'What?' he said, looking at Douglas. 'A child? They sent a child to fight me?'

'I am no child, you big ugly ogre,' said Douglas.

'Right lad! I am going to wipe the floor with you and throw your dead body to the wolves!' warned Big Gordon.

'I don't think so,' said Douglas, pulling out his catapult and loading it with a stone. 'This very day I will chop off your head.'

Big Gordon roared with laughter. 'You don't even have a sword you little squirt!'

Douglas aimed the catapult at Big Gordon. It never entered Big Gordon's head that such a small opponent could beat him. Unfortunately, for Big Gordon, what did enter his head was the pebble that Douglas catapulted at him. It hit him right in the forehead, killing him first time. He slumped to the ground and breathed his last.

A cheer went up from the Mancunians. Their opponents watched open mouthed as Douglas took Big Gordon's sword and cut off his head. He held it up for the Mancunians, who cheered and rushed forward towards the enemy lines. The enemy realised the fight was lost, and fled away, pursued by the Mancunians.

That day, in every home in Manchester, the story was told of Douglas Fairhurst and his victory at the battle of Warrington. Mayor Stewart Ogden gave

Douglas a job leading some of the armies of the city, and his fame spread across the land.

Several years later, Stewart Ogden was charged with corruption and fell from office. After the case was over, the people of Manchester duly elected Douglas Fairhurst as their new Mayor. And under his leadership the city prospered once more.

17

The Bad Sheila Affair

It was soft boiled eggs and toasted soldiers for breakfast at Brookdale Hall. Godfrey had stayed overnight after visiting the day before. They talked long into the night about important matters. The Father and the Son ate breakfast in silence.

Sunbeams poured into the dining room on this crisp but sunny autumn morning. Godfrey looked out of the window. A low mist hung across the lawns.

Jack had finished his two eggs and was spreading butter and marmalade onto a slice of toast. He took a swig of his coffee.

'I've got young Eric, the junior angel, coming for nineteen holes on the putting green this morning.' said Jack.

'Ah, the putting green.' said Godfrey. 'I'll be walking by there shortly, to the back gate.'

'You're using the tradesmen's entrance this morning then, Dad!' said Jack.

Godfrey smiled, still looking out of the window. He

poured a final mug of tea and got up from the table.

'I'm sorry about last night, Jack,' he said.

'Dad, it's all right. You did not put anything on me. I took something on myself. At the right time, the Cancer Tree will have to be dealt with. I have often asked you how we could destroy it. You explained that in detail last night. No one can take my life from me, Dad. I will lay it down of my own accord. I will lay it down and then take it up again.'

Godfrey kept his gaze towards the window so that Jack would not see the tear that ran down his face. He took a swig of tea and discretely wiped the tear away with the back of his hand.

'Right, I am off then, Son.'

Jack came over to the window behind Godfrey and put his hands on his shoulders. 'Stay peaceful, Dad.' Jack rested his head on Godfrey's shoulder. 'Don't let them boggarts get to you.'

Godfrey put his hand on Jack's head. 'I will stay peaceful, Son. I will.'

There was a knock at the door and a voice called out.

'Ay up!' It was Eric, the junior angel. 'Ready to be defeated?' he asked with a smile.

Jack laughed. 'Yeah, because that's me – always defeated!'

As he went to greet Eric, Jack looked back at Godfrey. 'We will not be defeated, Dad,' he said with a smile.

Godfrey's heart was heavy but he appreciated his son's assurance. He collected the breakfast things and took them to the kitchen to wash them up. Jack and Eric walked down to the old shed on the putting green to choose their putters for the game. Jack reached into an empty paint tin in the corner, and pulled out a couple of golf balls. 'Let's do it!' said Eric, leading the way to the starting point.

As Eric teed up his ball for the first hole, Jack looked across to the bottom of the green. He saw the lonely figure of Godfrey make his way to the back edge of Brookdale then disappear through the narrow back gate.

'Yay! Hole-in-one!' shouted Eric, punching the air.

'Steady on, Eric,' said Jack laughing. 'Start too strong and the only way is down. I'm planning to fail for the first half of the game. Then I'll come from nowhere and surprise you.'

Eric was far too excited at his hole-in-one to notice the profound statement Jack had just made.

Godfrey walked up the little dirt track that ran along the boundary of Jack's Brookdale estate. A little terrace of four cottages lined the track up to old Sam's house. The occupants were busy weaving cloth on handlooms in the workroom at the back of each dwelling. Just beyond the terrace was a larger house standing on its own. Godfrey opened the little red gate and admired the roses growing in the front garden. He knocked on the red door and waited.

'This is what I do,' muttered Godfrey to himself, and he started to smile. 'I stand at the door and knock. If anyone opens the door I will come in and have a brew.'

Eventually, he heard someone undoing the catch on the door.

'Hang on!' came a muffled voice from inside.

The door opened and there stood Ada Knott – a grey-haired old lady with a warm smile.

'Ay up! Here's trouble!' said Ada, laughing and giving Godfrey a hug and a peck on the cheek.

'Is the prophet Sam in?' asked Godfrey.

'Aye, he's just out in the back yard. Come in love. I was just doing Sam a brew and a jam butty. Do you want one?'

'That'll be lovely, Ada,' said Godfrey.

She led Godfrey into the back kitchen where the kettle was coming to the boil. Opening the back door she shouted 'Sam! Tea up! And you've got a visitor!'

She made a few jam butties and put them on a plate.

'Come through,' she said to Godfrey, leading him back to the front room.

They sat together by a small coal fire and were soon joined by Sam.

'Ay up! How are you my friend?' said Sam, entering the room. Sam wore an old jacket and trousers, and a flat cap to keep his bald head warm.

As the three of them tucked into jam butties and had a brew, Godfrey caught up with their news and then shared the reason for his visit.

Sam Knott was Douglas Fairhurst's oldest friend and most faithful advisor. But since Douglas had become Mayor of Manchester his visits had become less frequent.

'Interesting,' said Godfrey. 'His visits to me have become less frequent too.'

'He's a good lad,' said Sam, with his usual wisdom. 'But the pressure of high office makes most people become self-reliant or arrogant. Douglas has transformed our city to the extent that some refer to it as the

'City of Douglas' these days.'

'He is a good lad,' agreed Godfrey. 'A man after my own heart. I love him like a son. But he keeps trying to impress the people, and me, with his elaborate projects. I don't need to be impressed. I could not love him more than I already do. But if he keeps trying to out-perform himself and others, he'll burn out and shipwreck his life.'

Sam looked at the coal fire and pondered.

'He's going to bring Martin's piano back,' said Ada.

'Aye,' said Sam. 'Bringing Martin Simmonite's piano back from Urmston with brass bands and marching troops. There's going to be a big party at Platt Fields Park and everything.'

'Hmmm,' said Godfrey. 'What will that achieve?'

'Well that piano does carry such a history,' said Ada, slurping tea from her saucer.

'Exactly,' said Godfrey. 'It will stir the people and raise support. But I am concerned about what is happening in the heart of that young man – from shepherd boy to successful Mayor in a couple of leaps. He doesn't write music anymore. He was better when he was more creative. Now it seems it's all about keeping the 'Legend of Douglas' alive.'

'It could all end in tears,' said Ada, biting into her butty.

'Well I am always here for him,' said Sam.

'Me too,' said Godfrey. 'I just hope ...' His voice trailed off.

Sam and Ada looked at Godfrey, who was staring into the fireplace.

'Well, I've got some jobs calling me in the

backyard,' said Sam, breaking the silence.

'Aye, and I need to get me housework done,' said Ada.

'Yes. Well thanks for your time and the brew, and the butty,' said Godfrey. 'Let's hope Douglas remembers his roots.'

Godfrey said goodbye to Sam and Ada and walked back down the dirt track to Brookdale. The mist had cleared and the sun was shining. He walked through the narrow gate.

'Loser!' said Eric, shouting at the nineteenth hole.

'Yes I am,' said Jack smiling. 'I always become the loser so others can become winners.'

Again, Eric was too busy punching the air to understand the power of Jack's statement.

Godfrey met with the pair of contenders.

'I won again!' said Eric, smiling at Godfrey. He didn't have it in his heart to tell Eric that it was always in Jack's nature to lose, so that others could win.

'You did indeed, Eric,' said Godfrey. 'How did that happen?'

Jack shot a smile at Godfrey.

Godfrey winked.

Pudding People

An ancient tribe of people from the North East, famous for their batter puddings and roast beef. See also 'Yorkshire.'

oOo

It was a time of war between the people of Lancashire and the Pudding People on the East side of the Mountains of Ninepence. But this particular year, Douglas Fairhurst didn't feel like going to war. He had everything he wanted anyway. What could possibly be gained from another battle?

He was sitting in the roof garden of his Mayoral mansion in Didsbury and basking in the glory of the party a few weeks ago. At Platt Fields Park, thousands of residents of Manchester had gone wild for Douglas, who had brought back Martin Simmonite's piano from Urmston. It hadn't been stolen; it had just been forgotten and stored at the house of a relative.

Not only had he performed some of his new songs on his ukulele, but the crowd were delirious when brass-band processions led the way for Martin's piano to be carried forward. When Douglas played three historic songs, followed by one of his own songs, the crowd was ecstatic. The city was alive with the buzz of the day.

Now it was a warm summer evening with a glorious sky. He took another swig of red wine as he lay on a lounger, and felt pleased with himself.

He stood up and walked to the edge of the roof, looking towards the city centre. Birds were singing. He was buzzing. Almost everything was good. Life was mostly good. However, he had been having some family problems recently and his wife had gone away for a long weekend to 'get some space.' He was great at public and political relationships, but he was not so good with personal relationships.

In his darkest moments, he dreamed of his wife

having a tragic accident and dying, so that he would be free to remarry, without his public persona suffering. But this dark fantasy never happened.

He looked to the horizon. Then he made a mistake. He looked down. He could see most of his neighbour's garden, and, on this fateful night his neighbour's wife lying out by the pool in a very small bikini.

'Oh-my-giddy-aunt!' he muttered under his breath. His gaze was locked on the vision of femininity stretched out below. For what seemed an age, he stared. He drooled.

When she turned over and lay on her back, Douglas dropped his glass.

His mouth began to move but no sound came out. Gradually he regained some control of his basic functions and went to the stairs. He leaned into the stairwell.

'Charlie! Charlie!' he shouted down, to his personal assistant.

Charlie came running up the stairs thinking an emergency had occurred.

'What is it Douglas?'

The pair walked over to the edge of the roof garden and looked down on the female form.

'Who ...' began Douglas. 'Who ... who is that?'

'That is Sheila,' said Charlie.

Douglas looked at Charlie.

'She is the wife of Arnold,' said Charlie.

Douglas looked at Charlie with a sort of gormless face.

'Arnold - one of your chief commanders, who you sent to fight the Pudding People on the Mountains of Ninepence.

'Oh, right, him,' said Douglas, still staring and drooling at the vision of beauty below.

'Well, as she is sacrificing the company of her husband for our cause tonight, we should entertain her,' said Douglas unconvincingly.

Charlie looked with curiosity at Douglas.

'Dinner, Charlie. Go and invite her for dinner.'

'What date shall I suggest, Sir?'

'Date? No date. Now! Invite her to come now, Charlie!'

Charlie was used to Douglas' impulses and went off to see if the neighbour was interested. The thing is, Douglas was the famous Mayor of Manchester, and pretty much every one of his neighbours was always available to accept an invite to the Mayor's mansion. Every one of them had aspired, and worked, and toiled, and even cheated, to live near the famous Mayor Douglas. Arnold, on the other hand, came to live next door to Douglas because he was a successful commander of the army of Douglas. Yet Douglas had never noticed him.

However, Douglas had certainly noticed Arnold's wife. Within the hour, she was having dinner on the roof garden with Douglas. Charlie served the best champagne.

Sheila wore a slinky silver gown with a split up to her right thigh. An occasional flash of her formidable thigh, and a glimpse of her cleavage as she leaned forward when laughing at his jokes, and Douglas was besotted.

As the pair laughed and joked into the night, Douglas let Charlie go and rest. The couple were alone. The air was intoxicating to both of them. Sheila thought she may be paving the way for a promotion for her husband, whom she missed greatly. Douglas thought he had, at last, found his soul mate. Neither was true.

Nature, and alcohol, took their course. Two strangers, hungry for new adventures and the company of the opposite sex, let their guard down.

oOo

Three months later, Douglas and his wife sat out on the lawn of their Didsbury mansion, eating a fine breakfast of bacon and tomatoes on toast, when Charlie approached with some urgent news. He told Douglas that he had an important visitor.

'Show them in,' he said, waving his hand at Charlie.

'Erm, no Sir, they wish to speak with you privately.' Charlie was looking him in the eye.

Douglas had no idea what he was talking about but he knew a discrete signal when he saw one.

'Excuse me dear,' he said to his wife, who didn't even acknowledge his comment.

Once indoors, Charlie quietly briefed Douglas that Shelia was pregnant with his child.

'Are you sure it's mine?' asked Douglas. 'Well, Arnold is still on the front line on the Mountains of Ninepence,' said Charlie.

'Really?' said Douglas. 'Get him home! Send a messenger and tell him he has a few nights leave.'

Within a couple of days, Arnold was back. But he didn't quite go home. When Douglas asked about his arrival, Charlie informed him of the situation.

'Well, Sir, Arnold is committed to his men. And he says that while they are all roughing it in tents on the hills, he will also rough it in a tent; as they are missing their wives, he will keep himself from his wife also.'

'Bugger,' said Douglas. 'Can't you convince him to sleep with his own wife?'

'I'm afraid not, Sir,' said Charlie.

Douglas had hoped that by bringing Arnold back, he would have slept with his wife and assumed the pregnancy was his own doing. A scandal of adultery could bring his Mayoral career crashing down. He could not risk that.

He didn't sleep that night, and in the morning, the worse for wear, he instructed a messenger to carry a secret message to Arnold's superiors. Arnold was returning to them and they were to locate the fiercest part of the battle in the war, and send Arnold to the front line. When fighting broke out, they were to abandon him. This they did. As a result, Arnold died in action. Douglas had saved his reputation and his political career, but he was never at peace with himself after that day.

18

Old Sam goes to town

The prophet Sam left his home near Brookdale early next morning. He walked down by the canal all the way to Manchester. He called at the office of the Mayor. He was a familiar face to all the Mayor's staff and they showed him up to the Mayor's private office, where Douglas stood, looking out of the window.

'Ah Sam. Come in, Old Boy. Nice to see you,' he said.

His secretary bought a pot of tea and some biscuits.

'I've come to ask your advice, Lad' said Sam.

'Oh?' said Douglas. 'It is usually me asking you for advice.'

'There are two men in town, one is rich and the other is poor. The rich man has a very large number of sheep and cows, but the poor man has nothing except one little lamb that he bought. He raised it, and it grew up with him and his children. It shared his food, drank from his cup and even slept in his arms; it was like a daughter to him. Now, a traveller came to the rich man, but the rich man didn't take one of his own sheep or cows to prepare a meal for him. Instead, he took the lamb that belonged to the poor man.' Douglas became angry about the man.

'The man who did this deserves jail! He must pay for that lamb four times over, because he did such a thing and had no pity.'

'You are the man!' said Sam.

Douglas froze. His mouth dropped open.

'Godfrey made you Mayor of Manchester, and he delivered you from the hand of Big Gordon. He gave you a big house and a beautiful wife. He gave you the land of Manchester and Lancashire. And if all this had been too little, he would have given you even more. What you have done is not right. You arranged the death of Arnold and took his wife to be your own. You killed him with the sword of the Pudding People. Therefore trouble shall never leave your house. You have welcomed the spirit of death and the spirit of the boggarts into your affairs. How can things go well if you do that?'

Sam's words were like a sharp sword in Douglas' heart. His old friend had spoken the truth. Douglas wept bitterly.

'Sam! What have I done? I have taken everything Godfrey gave me and ruined it by always having my own way. I'm finished if Godfrey has abandoned me!'

'He has not abandoned you. He never will,' said Sam. 'He sent me here to prepare you for tears. The first half of your life was a life of laughter. But this second part of your life will be filled with tears. You scooped fire into your lap and thought your clothes would not burn. But they did. If you renew your friendship with Godfrey, his wisdom will dwell in you. Life will be better for you.'

Douglas thanked Sam for his visit and became a changed man. He was more humble after that day.

A few months later, Sheila gave birth to their son. But the boy was sick from birth. Douglas did everything he could to save the little boy. But the boy died. He and Sheila wept bitter tears as they grasped his ghost.

When his wife left him that same year, Douglas wept again. Soon afterwards he married Sheila in a discreet ceremony and she moved in to the Didsbury mansion.

oOo

The wind and rain whipped across the hills as Douglas climbed the slopes of Lily Lane towards Hartshead Pike. Now and then the odd hailstone would sting his face but Douglas pressed on. He was cold and wet but he was on a mission. The turmoil of the climate was nothing compared to the turmoil that raged in his heart.

In his mind, he was rehearsing his apology to Godfrey and hoping all was not lost. It would never be like before, but perhaps he could just work for Godfrey or do something that might impress him. Perhaps he would build a cathedral in Godfrey's honour. As soon as he entered the narrow gate the rain and wind stopped. He looked up to Godfrey's tower. He swallowed hard. His heart pounded in his chest. And then he saw Godfrey, running down the hill to meet him. He was confused. Was Godfrey coming to take revenge on him? He stood his ground. Whatever lecture, condemnation or punishment was coming, he was guilty. He knew that. Whatever it was, he deserved it. And again his heart wrestled to think of something he could do to redeem himself.

When Godfrey reached him he embraced him like a long lost friend.

'You came home! Oh Douglas, I have missed you!'

Overwhelmed by the torrent of love and forgiveness flowing from Godfrey, Douglas burst into tears.

'I'm sorry! I am so, so sorry Godfrey. I took all the good things you gave me and now I have ruined everything!'

'It's all right Douglas. Be at peace, Lad.' Godfrey pulled his head to his. 'You're home now.'

After a few moments of tears and embracing, the pair climbed on, up to Godfrey's tower. 'I'll make it up to you somehow, Godfrey.'

There, by the coal fire, were dry clothes for Douglas, including a very expensive suit, which Godfrey had laid out ready.

'There you are lad. Take them and go and get changed in the spare room.'

Douglas was still waiting for the condemning lecture, but it never came. He got changed and washed the tears from his face. He rejoined Godfrey by the fireplace.

'Something smells nice,' said Douglas.

'Shepherd's pie – your favourite I believe?' said Godfrey, with a twinkle in his eye.

'Yes it is. Are you expecting company then?'

'Yes. You! I made it for you. We shall open a fine bottle of red wine, and there is trifle for afters.'

'I don't understand.'

'Dear Douglas, I thought you were dead to me. I thought you had thrown your lot in with the boggarts. But you haven't. You heard my voice drawing you here, and you came home. That is all my heart wanted from you. You were lost but now you are found. You were dead but now you are alive! Your spirit is alive Douglas!'

Not for the last time that day, Douglas felt overwhelmed by Godfrey's gentleness and generosity.

The pair sat down to dinner. Godfrey dished up the shepherd's pie to the former shepherd boy.

'I am going to build you a palace in the heart of Manchester, and a cathedral and a statue and everything!'

'No, Douglas. No, you are not. Have I ever asked for such things?'

'Well, no. But I can do it. I want to do it.'

'You know, Douglas, this is your real problem. You think you need to earn my approval and love. You don't. I have been besotted with you since the day you were conceived. It is not possible for me to love you more than I already do.

For you, it seems all about performance. But it isn't. Really it isn't. You seem to think that the problem between me and humans can be fixed by you, from your side. Well, here's a newsflash for you, action man – it cannot. It can only be fixed by me from my side and I am going to fix it when the time is right.'

'Well, just what exactly shall I do then?.

'There you go again, Lad. 'Do?' Why do you feel the need to 'do' something? I made you a human being not a human doing. It is really about who you should be. And the answer to that is to be true to yourself, true to your heart and true to your family. Let my spirit flow in your spirit, and keep your heart soft towards me. When you do that, everything else will fall into place. Here endeth the lesson.'

Douglas glanced over to a huge sherry trifle on the sideboard.

'Yes. Time for afters!' said Godfrey, clearing the plates into the kitchen. He came back with two large dishes and a big spoon. Soon the pair fell silent as the glory of the trifle tickled every taste bud.

After dinner the friends returned to the fireside and Godfrey smoked his pipe. Douglas began to relax even though his planned speech of repentance was still running through his head.

'Douglas, I know it's in your heart to build a cathedral and a palace in my honour. But that will not be your work. I will provide a good place for you and your people, rather than you providing a place for me.

One day a cathedral and a palace will be built in Manchester. But they will be built by a son not yet born to you; a son that will succeed you as Mayor when you have faded from view and gone to rest with your fathers. I will be like a father to him, and he shall be like my son.'

Douglas was deeply moved. He did have a desire for a building in his heart. And his heart was still broken because of the death of his baby son. But now Godfrey had spoken of another son who would build what was in his heart.

A tear rolled down Douglas' cheek and his lip quivered a little.

'Brandy is what we chiefly need,' said Godfrey,

squeezing Douglas' shoulder as he went to get the drinks.

'Not for me, Godfrey. I have had more than enough of everything tonight.'

'More than enough? Ha ha! It's called abundance! It was my plan all along for you humans.'

Douglas hugged Godfrey. 'Goodnight my dear friend.'

'Sleep well, son.'

Godfrey settled by the fire to watch the flames dance. Within the hour, he was sleeping soundly. Outside on the hills an owl hooted in the darkness as the Northern drizzle cloaked the landscape.

19

A most expensive pearl

Raindrops were poking rings into the puddles at Brookdale Park. Godfrey and Jack were sitting by the big window in the dining room, eating fish and chips and mushy peas. They looked out of the window at the gloomy sky.

'You know, we really must get that broken stopcock fixed at Woodhead. If we're not careful, they'll be another flood, Dad,' said Jack.

'No. I can promise you that will not happen again,' said Godfrey looking pensive.

A rainbow appeared in the sky.

'Oh this fish is the best I've ever tasted!' said Jack. 'It's the piece of cod that passes understanding.'

Godfrey rolled his eyes.

'You know there is one thing we haven't tried,' said Godfrey.

'What's that, Dad?' asked Jack, throwing a chip in the air and catching it in his mouth.

'Well, we have never really given any human everything they wanted and more, have we?' said Godfrey.

'Erm ... didn't you start this whole thing by giving Albert and Edna everything they wanted and more?' asked Jack.

'That is true,' said Godfrey, taking a swig of dandelion and burdock. 'But that was before the Cancer Tree took effect. What I mean is, what if we gave one human everything they could want and then some? What if we made one of them rich beyond their wildest dreams?'

'Hmmm? Not sure,' said Jack, dipping a chip butty into his mushy peas. 'Can you think of any really rich people who stayed in touch with us? Think of all the people who discover the narrow gate and wander up here. They tend to be poor, broken, depressed, or killers on the run. We don't get many rich and successful people coming for dinner do we?'

'What we need,' said Godfrey, 'is to have someone who'll stay close to us and marries someone who'll stay close to us, so their children will tend to stay close to us. The trouble always comes when people marry followers of boggarts. They get dragged down into all sorts of darkness and pain.'

'Well it could be worth a try, Dad.'

Jack mopped up the last of his mushy peas with a slice of bread and butter. 'What about the baby that Douglas and Sheila Fairhurst had a while back?'

'Who? Little Simon Fairhurst?' asked Godfrey.

'That's the little chap!' said Jack. 'He'll need to be rich if he's the one going to build the cathedral and the palace in Manchester.'

'That's true. You do keep saying things that are true, Son.'

'Hey, I am the Truth!' said Jack laughing.

Godfrey put the last crispy bits of chip on a butty and bit into it. He watched a raindrop slide slowly down the window pane.

'Simon Fairhurst ...' he mumbled to himself, as Jack brought in a pot of tea and some chocolate biscuits.

oOo

Simon Fairhurst arrived at his jewellery shop in Didsbury at 8:30am as usual. The events of the day before were still playing in his head. All of Manchester and the surrounding districts had gathered at Platt Fields to mourn the death of his father. Douglas Fairhurst was a legend across Manchester. But after his seventieth birthday he became increasingly frail and ill and now, within a year, he had passed away.

Simon, the son of Douglas and Sheila, had been sworn in as the new Mayor of Manchester. He stood in awe of his father and the legacy he left across the North West.

At the funeral of Mayor Douglas, the one thing that troubled Simon was the lack of a grand venue for such state occasions. His father had spoken often of the need for a cathedral and a palace in Manchester. Something began to grow in Simon's heart – a desire to see those two buildings constructed in his lifetime.

As his civic duties increased, Simon had to give oversight of his chain of jewellery shops to a group of managers, so he could lead the people of Manchester.

The day after his father's funeral, Simon was on his final week of running his Didsbury store, and was training the new manager to take over this shop.

They were going through a large account book that

listed the current stock, when a man came into the shop. Simon looked over his glasses at the stranger, who looked out of place. He was some sort of tradesman - that was clear. He had a neat set of small screwdrivers sticking out of the chest pocket of his blue dungarees. He had long hair, a big smile and a flat carpenter's pencil tucked behind one ear.

Simon felt he needed to get this man out of the shop as soon as was politely possible.

'Can I help you Sir?'

'Pearls!' said the stranger staring Simon right in the eye.

'Pearls? Ah yes, here we are.'

Simon went to the budget end of the counter and opened the display to retrieve the cheapest pearl necklace he could find.

'How about these, Sir?'

'No, thanks. They look a bit cheap and nasty. Have you got something more expensive?'

Simon scanned the stranger once more, noticing bits of sawdust in his hair. He tried to hide his disdain.

He brought four more pearl necklaces and presented them to his customer.

'Still look a bit cheap.'

Simon was struggling to keep his composure. 'What are you looking for exactly, Sir?'

'Not a necklace really, just a single pearl.'

'And your budget, Sir? What price range are we thinking about?'

'Oh there is no price limit. In fact, the more expensive the better.'

The manager smiled unconvincingly at the stranger

as Simon went into the back room. He came back with a large pearl, on a purple cushion in a glass case.

'I think this may be what you want?' Simon took out the pearl and showed it to the man.

To his surprise, the man took out a small jeweller's lens and examined the pearl closely. He stroked his chin and looked at Simon.

'I can assure you this is the most expensive pearl on the premises, Sir.'

The stranger put the lens to his eye and looked at Simon through it.

'I don't think it is, young man.'

He put the lens back in his pocket and turned to go. Simon and the manager followed him with their gaze.

'I don't think it is,' he repeated, smiling when he got to the door. He winked at Simon and was gone.

oOo

When it came to jewellery, Simon knew his stuff. Being a jeweller came easy to him. It had been his life. But now he had stepped into his Dad's shoes, as it were, as Mayor of Manchester. The city was thriving and growing at an amazing rate. The population and the prosperity grew year on year. But Simon was uneasy. He didn't feel he had his father's leadership skills. He often thought of his Dad and the days before leadership had fallen onto his shoulders.

One day, he remembered an old man who used to come and visit when he had been little. Yes, old Sam Knott was his name. He seemed to give his Dad wisdom from time to time. Simon began asking around to see if he could locate the old prophet. One of the elderly cleaners at the council offices remembered old Sam.

'Aye Love,' she told him. 'He lived up in Newton Heath, just a short way from the canal. But he'd be ever so old if he's still alive.'

'Thank you, Madam,' said Simon.

Next morning Simon rode his horse up the towpath of the canal. It was still misty when he reached Newton Heath. He found the little dirt track at Stotts Lane, and rode slowly towards the place the cleaner had directed. He found the little bent dirt track and the house with the red door. But the windows were all smashed and the door was hanging by one hinge. He dismounted his horse and tied it to the fence. The place was eerily silent. Old Sam's house and the row of weavers' cottages all stood empty and derelict. Simon looked down the track to see where it led but he couldn't see for the mist. He walked onwards to explore, as his horse stooped to eat the grass near Old Sam's fence.

He came to a tall green fence, and followed it along to a small narrow gate. The word "Welcome" was painted in yellow.

Curious as to where the gate led, Simon pushed it open. Somehow, beyond the gate the mist was absent and the light much brighter. He squinted to see through the light and saw two figures playing golf.

'He shoots! He scores!' laughed the younger figure.

The gate squeaked loudly as it swung closed. The figures looked in Simon's direction. He felt guilty, as though he was trespassing, but the sign did say "Welcome."

One of the figures ran towards him laughing. 'Ha ha! There you are young Simon!'

Simon was confused. How did this stranger know his name?

'Welcome! Welcome!'

Godfrey hugged Simon like a long lost friend and walked with him towards the other figure as he continued to chat.

'This is our Jack,' said Godfrey. Simon offered his hand to shake but Jack gave him a bear hug.

'Come up to the house and we'll have lunch,' said Jack.

Simon kept looking at Jack – he seemed familiar.

At the house, the smell of roast beef and roast parsnips filled the air.

Simon began to realise who Godfrey was.

'Are you Godfrey – the Godfrey my Dad used to talk about?'

'Yes, indeed I am!' said Godfrey, showing Simon to his seat at the table.

As Eric, the junior angel, served lunch to the three of them, Simon looked across to Jack.

'You look familiar.'

'Got any expensive pearls?'

'Yes! You are the one – the one who came to my shop that day. I showed you the most expensive one I had.'

'No, you didn't really, Simon.'

'But I really did!'

'Ah Simon, I was looking for a priceless pearl, a very expensive one. I was looking for you.'

'What?'

'You. You are the priceless pearl I was looking for.

Or to be more precise, I was looking at you humans. Each one of you is an expensive pearl.'

Simon didn't understand.

'I am considering making the most expensive purchase of my life – I am prepared to give everything I have, if I can purchase the most expensive pearls for my wonderful Dad.'

Simon scratched his head, and began eating the amazing roast beef dinner that Eric had served up. Godfrey poured the three of them a small glass of claret as he explained why he had called Simon to him. 'Simon, I am going to give you anything you want. So while we are eating lunch, have a think. You are the leader of Manchester and the son of Douglas, my friend. Ask me for anything and I'll give it to you.'

The whole situation seemed surreal to Simon. Was he dreaming? As he mulled over Godfrey's offer, he knew the one thing he desired most was wisdom; as a powerful leader, people were asking him for many decisions to be made every day. Then there were the disputes that the local magistrates couldn't settle, which were also passed to Simon. This was one area where he felt very insecure. The fact that, so far, he had not made a disastrous decision was a thing of wonder to him. He felt it was only a matter of time.

'Let's have coffee and chocs on the lawn!' said Jack.

Philip and Eric set out a table and chairs on the lawn.

'Now, I've served the coffee and chocolate, but I hope you don't mind if Eric and I have angel cake,' said Philip.

'Of course,' said Jack. 'Feel free. I just want everyone to be free.'

'Now, young Simon, have you given my offer any

thought?' asked Godfrey.

'Yes I have,' said Simon. 'If possible, what I'd really like, if it's not too much trouble, is wisdom.'

Godfrey smiled and paused. He looked at the ground for a moment. He was a bit taken aback.

'So I offer you anything in the world, and you ask for wisdom?'

'If it is possible.'

'Everything is possible. That's my point. You didn't ask for great wealth, a long life, or the death of your enemies. You asked for wisdom. Young man, that is impressive.'

'Well, the truth is, Sir, I stand in the shadow of a legend. He was a great leader. They made a statue of him and everything. But I'm just a bloke. I know next to nothing about leading a city.'

'Well, Simon, because you have asked for wisdom, I am going to give you great wisdom. But more than that, I am also going to give you more wealth than any human has ever had. On top of that, I'm giving you honour and fame. In your lifetime there will be no equal to you.

But there is one thing I ask; keep your heart soft towards me. If you keep an ear open to my voice, and your gaze towards my light, you will also have a long life. Keep connected to me Simon, that it may go well for you.'

Once again that day, Simon Fairhurst was taken aback. He was still pondering what Jack had meant about him being the priceless pearl he had been looking for.

The warm sunshine, the roast dinner, the claret, and then coffee and chocolates began to take their toll; the chairs were very comfortable, the conversation stilled. The peacocks squawked in the distance as Godfrey, Jack, and Simon dozed in their chairs. Only Philip and Eric remained alert.

Simon woke with a start as his horse licked his face with its huge horse tongue. He was leaning against old Sam's derelict house. The mist had cleared and Simon assumed he had been dreaming. It was time to go home.

What a dream! As he rode down the canal towpath back to his home he felt very satisfied. He thought he'd be hungry by now but he wasn't. He licked the back of his teeth. There was a definite taste of chocolate.

20

The wise and foolish builder

Down at Boggart Hole Clough, in Blackley, Owd Hob climbed out of the hole leading from his underground castle. To most creatures this was not possible. Indeed, that is how so many humans and animals ended up on the dining table at Owd Hob's castle – they slid down the wet mossy hole to their death. It was only Owd Hob's slug-like skin that enabled him to climb the slimy walls.

A coach and horses driven by two Jack o' lanterns was waiting to transport him. Just like the horses, the coach was black as night. The horses wore black funeral plumes on their heads. The driving icy rain made Owd Hob smile. He hoped all Godfrey-lovers were suffering the biting cold. He climbed into the coach, which was more like a hearse, and stretched out in the vacant coffin. He smiled again. He loved the smell of death. As he held the side of the coffin his slimy excretions dribbled down the outside of it. The Jack o' lanterns cracked the whip and the horses jumped into action.

As they travelled down the road, Owd Hob laughed at a small boy screaming as the local dentist extracted an abscessed tooth without anaesthetic. He looked across to the local schoolyard to see another small boy being violently beaten by five other boys.

'Wonderful! Wonderful!' he laughed to himself. Yes, his spells - to cause as much pain and suffering to humans as possible - were most effective in the areas where he ruled.

The coach drove on towards Harpurhey. When he passed by Moston Cemetery, Owd Hob sniffed the air. 'I love the stench of death!' he laughed, as he surveyed the seemingly endless graves, some of which had been vandalised.

About half a mile past the cemetery, the coach turned left. The houses disappeared and they entered a dark wood. What at first looked like decaying leaves on the ground were actually rotting cigarette ends. The air was filled with the smell of stale tobacco and alcohol. Now the trees resembled empty wine bottles, crowded together. And there, in the middle of Green Glass Wood, stood Winterdyne Cottage – a large ancient house.

The Jack o' lanterns stopped the coach at the door of the cottage. Owd Hob sniffed the stale air. His snake-like tongue flicked in and out, seeming to taste the stench. He climbed down from the coach and banged on the front door.

A thin, weak-looking man answered the door, his black hair parted exactly in the middle. He stared at Owd Hob with his large eyes.

'Oh it's you,' said Harold, looking disappointed.

'Yes, it is me!' said Owd Hob.

'I'm sure Karen will be pleased to see you,' said Harold, scowling.

In the back room the ceiling was painted dark green and the walls were deep purple. A witch's broom lay on top of the bookcase. And there, on the red velvet sofa, was Karen clothed in black. Dark hair framed her face and her eyes lit up at the sight of her visitor. She jumped up and embraced the chief of the boggarts.

'Oooh! Naughty Hob!' she said, as Owd Hob grasped her backside and his snake-like tongue flicked in her ear.

'Harold! Open the wine and empty the ashtray!' commanded Karen.

Harold did as he was told. He appeared to be more of a butler but, truth be told, he was Karen's long-suffering husband. Her many affairs had wearied him, but Harold still held on to the hope that Karen would one day love him again.

'Karen, I need you ...' began Owd Hob.

'Oh lucky me!' said Karen, running her finger across his shoulder.

Harold scowled again.

'Go and buy me some fags!' Karen yelled at Harold.

He knew his place. There were plenty of cigarettes in the house. He knew this was a signal for him to disappear for an hour.

Karen opened a packet of cigarettes and lit up. She pulled the nearest ashtray onto the arm of the sofa, pulled her feet up, and sat in a provocative pose maintaining eye contact with Owd Hob.

'I need you to advise me,' said Owd Hob. 'Godfrey has installed a new man in charge of the city. It seems this man is of a very rare breed of leader – he has integrity!'

'No! Integrity? That died out years ago!' laughed Karen.

'Apparently not,' said Owd Hob. 'Godfrey offered this guy anything he wanted ... and this guy asked for ... wisdom!'

'No way!' said Karen. 'You're joking!'

'I wish,' said Owd Hob, looking at Karen. 'I need you to break that integrity thing.'

'Easy!' said Karen. 'Especially for anyone in any sort of powerful position.'

'I'd hoped you'd say that,' said Hob.

'It's sex! Men in power cannot resist sex. I could bring him down tomorrow,' said Karen.

'I'm sure you could my dear,' said Owd Hob. 'But I want you to do it slowly, and pounce at the exact time that will be strategic for me. I want maximum damage and maximum disappointment to Godfrey.'

'No problem,' said Karen. 'I'll apply the pressure slowly and then, when you give me the command, he will fall like a house of cards.'

Before Harold returned, Owd Hob had satisfied himself with Karen in more ways than one. At the door he pulled Karen tightly toward him as he left.

'Don't fail me!' he demanded.

'Trust me,' she said, as she finished buttoning up her blouse.

Owd Hob stared and his snake-like tongue flicked about again. He climbed onto the coach and sat in the coffin. He smiled at Karen and waved his hand. The Jack o' lanterns cracked the whip, and the horses leapt into action.

The dark sky rumbled with thunder, and a lightning bolt struck a tree sending it crashing to the ground. Karen smiled and closed the door.

oOo

The next decade was one of massive and prolonged construction, as Simon Fairhurst began work on the cathedral, down by the River Irwell. The spires rose high above the normal buildings of Manchester. On the day of dedication, the whole city came out to see the cathedral.

There were grand processions of brass bands and local organisations along all major routes. From Oldham and Stockport, Trafford and Salford.

Martin Simmonite's piano was brought in a procession to the cathedral and given pride of place. Everyone cheered as the piano came on its special cart through the streets.

Simon played the piano and sang the old songs that his father had written about Godfrey. His son had built the temple, just as Godfrey had promised.

While everyone was singing, a white cloud appeared inside the cathedral, and everyone felt Godfrey was near.

Not content with the cathedral in Godfrey's honour, Simon cleared a large area in the city centre and built a huge triangular palace for himself, as Mayor of Manchester. In front of the palace, Simon created a civic square so people could appreciate the building. He named the square after the first human Godfrey had created – Albert .

Simon Fairhurst became so rich and powerful, that kings, queens, politicians and other great leaders came from far and wide to see the palace and the cathedral. Something happened to Simon in those days. He began to feel so proud of himself he lost touch with Godfrey. At the same time, he discovered a weakness for women. It was rooted in his feelings of inadequacy compared to his legendary father. He could never believe he was so powerful. Every day he assumed this inadequacy would be revealed and it would all be over. Yet, as each day passed, he only gained more wealth and power. Something inside him compelled him to maximise his own pleasure while it lasted.

His wife came home one day to find him in bed with another woman. And strangely, as Simon was so skilled in political speeches, he eventually convinced his wife that the affair was a good thing. Before long, he had a third woman on the go and again convinced his wife and his mistress that this was a good thing too.

By the end of the year, he had convinced the government to change the law to allow a man to have more than one wife. This opened the floodgates to his sexual activities and he found that he was insatiable. Within a few years he had seven hundred wives and three hundred mistresses.

One day during a private soiree with his latest mistresses, James, his private secretary, came in and notified him of an important visitor.

The Queen of Sheffield was en route and would be officially arriving at nine o'clock the following morning. Simon thanked James for the message and then waved him out the door, asking not to be disturbed for the rest of the day. The party with the women continued into the night.

Early next morning, a procession of camels came to Manchester carrying the Queen of Sheffield and her considerable entourage. Simon had heard of the legend of the Queen of Sheffield. Some said she was half human and half boggart. Simon was fascinated to meet this legend at last.

On her arrival, she was taken to the palace and introduced to Simon. He had never seen such a beautiful woman in his life. He became immediately besotted with her. She was also fascinated with Simon, having heard of his legendary wisdom and wealth. That night, there was an official reception and the pair got to know each other over dinner. He had many wives and mistresses, but he felt he could not have deep conversation with any of them, as his intellect was so much more developed. But here, in this strange visitor, he found not only incredible beauty but also an incredible intellect.

The following week, the couple spent all the time they could together. Simon was entranced. Not only was the Queen of Sheffield beautiful and intelligent, she was also virtuous. She would not be seduced by Simon's powers of persuasion. This made her even more desirable to him.

The Queen and her advisors stayed at the palace for six months. When she announced that she would be leaving to return to Sheffield, Simon begged her to stay one more day. And on the final night, after dinner, she fell for his charms. She could resist his advances no longer. They spent the night in his master bedroom.

The following morning, the camels were prepared and the Queen and her entourage left Manchester for Sheffield. Simon never saw her again. And he was never the same again. He pined for her every day.

Cracks began to appear in his leadership. He had forgotten about Godfrey all together. A few years later, one of his closest advisors overthrew him and took power. With his wealth and power gone, few people were interested in him anymore.

He retired to a small terrace house in Miles Platting where he lived alone. He died shortly after his sixty-ninth birthday, alone in his bed. Six of his former wives were the only ones who attended his funeral. He was laid to rest in Moston Cemetery.

21

The swarm of locusts

The Green boggart of Moss Side was anxious on this crisp autumnal night. He was expecting a visitor. As he looked to the horizon he saw dark billowing clouds move across the sky at Hulme. Owd Hob was approaching.

The Green boggart was fearful. He well remembered the Yellow boggart of Droylsden, who had disappointed their Master. Owd Hob had been so enraged that he blew a white-hot flame, which engulfed the Yellow boggart, his wife, and his Jack o' lantern. They were never seen or heard from again.

The Green boggart lived down a secret hole at Pepperhill Farm in Moss Side. Owd Hob passed the black and white timber house the farmer lived in, and drove on down to the boggart hole.

When the black hearse and horses pulled up, the Green boggart trembled with fear. Owd Hob jumped from his coffin, in the back of the hearse, and looked at the Green boggart with disdain.

'Have you done your work?' demanded Owd Hob.

'Yes, Master. I hope it is to your satisfaction,' stammered the Green boggart.

Owd Hob scowled at the boggart.

'Show me!'

The pair went down the boggart hole, followed by Owd Hob's Jack o' lanterns. There in the dimly lit workshop was an old table and on it stood three glass tanks, each containing six pregnant locusts.

Owd Hob stooped and looked at the locusts closely.

'Excellent. And they all have the secret virus?' asked Owd Hob.

'Yes, Master,' said the Green boggart nervously.

Owd Hob picked up the middle tank and nodded to his Jack o' lanterns to get the other two. Owd Hob chuckled as they marched back up to the surface. Back in the hearse, they set off towards Whalley Range. The Green boggart was still unsure if his Master was happy, but at least the visit was over.

At Whalley Range the driver halted the horses. Owd Hob climbed down from the hearse holding one of the glass tanks. He motioned to the Jack o' lanterns to join him with the other glass tanks. It was four o'clock in the morning and every human was sound asleep in their bed.

He looked into the darkness for a moment and smiled. He closed his eyes and then lifted the first glass tank above his head. The pregnant locusts became alert. He threw the glass tank hard towards the ground.

'Six!' shouted Owd Hob as the pregnant locusts were released from captivity.

He repeated this action with the remaining two glass tanks.

'Six! Six! Six!' he shouted into the darkness.

The locusts leapt across the ground into the night.

Owd Hob climbed back into the hearse and laughed all the way back to Blackley.

No human witnessed that incident in the dark hours. But soon every living thing felt the effect. The eighteen pregnant locusts gave birth to countless offspring. The locust swarm spread out to the four corners of Lancashire. The virus they carried silenced Godfrey's voice in the hearts of humans. On that day, the light of life went out of men and women. Violence increased across the land. Milk went sour. Women miscarried. Accidents increased. Children were orphaned. Human tears flowed like a river.

Down in Boggart Hole Clough, Owd Hob pulled the cork on a bottle of fermented vinegar he had been saving for a special occasion. He poured himself a large glass.

'Excellent. Excellent,' he said, as he downed the acidic brew.

The toll of human suffering was beyond reckoning. Jack moved back in with Godfrey at the tower at Hartshead Pike; Owd Hob led a team of boggarts to demolish Jack's house at Brookdale. As the great hall was reduced to rubble, Owd Hob laughed.

As suffering increased and the love of many grew cold, humans began to blame all the suffering and death on Godfrey. Owd Hob's plan was complete. Godfrey's creation had now felt the force of Owd Hob's rebellion, and most people were unaware of what they were up against.

As the lights went out across Lancashire, Godfrey stood outside his tower with Jack. It was so dark.

Hardly a star shone in the sky. Godfrey wept as he looked towards Manchester. Jack also wept as he hugged his Dad. Composing himself, Godfrey looked towards the horizon and thought of the original pair he had created – Albert and Edna. He thought of all their descendants with their hopes, and dreams, and human flaws.

The light of Sophia seemed to illuminate Godfrey and Jack, in the midst of the darkness.

Godfrey wiped his eyes, and at that moment, he made a promise to the humans he had created and declared it into the night.

'I will repay you for the years the locusts have eaten.'

It was also a promise to Owd Hob. One was a promise of restoration, the other a promise of retribution.

22

The Prophet Malarkey

During the dark days of the locust swarm, Italy invaded the land. Forces swept through every town in Lancashire and beyond. They captured Manchester and built a great fort there. They renamed the city 'Mancunia'. They built temples to honour themselves; men and women were worshipped like gods.

Under the Italian occupation, life became hard for the people of Manchester and Lancashire. These were dark and violent times. Italian brutality seemed to know no limits. Anyone who disobeyed the Italian rulers was either imprisoned or publicly executed.

One dark and lonely night, Murray Malarkey was walking steadily - his face set like flint. He was an old, thin Scotsman, with pointed features and wide eyes. His grey hair was thinning yet still wild. He was wrapped in a tartan cloak, and walked with a staff in his hand.

The rain beat down on his face as if to discourage him. But nothing would have stopped his Scottish determination that night. He approached Hartshead Pike. The swirling rain and wind seemed troubled by his presence on the hillside. He came to the wall at the bottom of the hill and found the narrow gate. His heart pounded in his chest as he looked towards the dark tower. A small candle flickered in a window.

Murray Malarkey stepped through the gate and stood in Godfrey's field, legs slightly apart, and planted his staff firmly on the ground. He took a deep breath and then yelled with every fibre of his being.

'I call on the Most High Lord Godfrey – creator of Heaven and Earth! Come to your people! We need to see your face!'

At the top of the hill, the door of the tower opened and Godfrey popped his head out. He struggled to see the figure yelling at the bottom of the hill. It had been many summers since any human had visited Godfrey, due to the curse of the boggarts, and the locusts.

Godfrey pulled on his boots and ran down the hill to meet the old man, who was repeating his loud mantra.

'I call on the Most High Lord Godfrey – creator of Heaven and Earth! Come to your people! We need to see your face!'

Godfrey reached the old man and embraced him. The man was grateful but continued to cry out.

'We're doomed, Lord Godfrey. Aye, we are all doomed I tell ye! Come to your people I pray!'

'It's alright,' Godfrey assured him. 'Come up to the tower and get warm.'

Murray sat in awe by the roaring fire, having a wee dram of whisky as he was introduced to Jack. No other human knew about the visitor to Hartshead Pike that night.

Murray Malarkey stayed with Godfrey and Jack for

seven days. It took that long for Godfrey to convince the Prophet Malarkey that everyone was not doomed. Something happened in the heart of the prophet that week. He was transformed from a prophet of doom to a prophet of hope. And on the final day, he bid farewell to Godfrey and Jack and walked all the way to Manchester, with a spring in his step and a song in his heart. Spring was in the air, and life seemed to be flourishing in the hedgerows as he smiled and sang his way home.

To be sure, there had been several prophets of hope during the Italian occupation of Manchester. All of them had called on the people to remember the teaching of Martin Simmonite, and the ten tips for physical, mental and spiritual health from the plaques on his piano. Prophet Malarkey was the final prophet who spoke to the people, before Jack appeared in Manchester.

The Prophet Malarkey did a tour of the entire North West, giving lectures in town halls and other local venues.

He challenged his audience to stop dealing treacherously with one another, since they all had one creator.

He championed women's rights, and challenged men to stop divorcing their wives for no reason, leaving them in poverty.

He told the crowd to prepare the way for a visitation from a saviour, who would bring healing to people's lives. This saviour was going to deal with the boggarts, once and for all.

He spoke about the need to be givers and not takers – so that the poor and needy could be cared for.

Finally, he declared that Godfrey would rekindle love in families, and bring peace where there was discord.

A book was published containing transcripts of the Prophet Malarkey's lectures. He greatly affected all who met him – they saw something of Godfrey in him. He became a legend throughout the whole of Manchester.

At ninety-one years of age, the Prophet Malarkey passed away. He was buried in Southern Cemetery.

Four hundred years passed, and no one sought out Godfrey. The words of the Prophet Malarkey were mostly forgotten. The boggarts assumed victory was theirs. Babies were born. People married. Life went on, though the hearts of many became cold. The deep sadness had gripped everyone.

PART 2

The Newer Times

23

The road from Wigan

Sophia and Jack were having a game of Ludo in the front room at Hartshead Pike. The glorious smell of roast turkey was making them hungry.

'That smells fantastic, Dad!' said Jack.

'Right. Time to set the table I think,' called Godfrey from the kitchen.

Sophia and Jack cleared the table and put the Ludo back in its box on the shelf.

Soon the table was filled with a large roast turkey, stuffing, roast parsnips and carrots, sprouts, roast potatoes, Yorkshire pudding and a jug of the most amazing gravy.

Godfrey opened a bottle of claret and poured three glasses. A roaring log fire was in the hearth, bringing some winter warmth as the snow continued to fall outside the tower.

The balcony was decorated with holly and ivy.

'So, are you sure you want to do this Jack?' asked Godfrey.

'Want? It is more that I have to do this, Dad. Four hundred years have passed since the Prophet Malarkey visited this tower. From then until now, not one human has found us. Four hundred years of silence, Dad! This problem cannot be fixed by them, from their side. We need to rescue the humans from the deception of Owd Hob, and the boggarts.'

'But the cost Jack ...'

'I know. I'll give it everything I've got.'

'That's what I am afraid of.'

Sophia was silent and dipped a roast potato in her gravy.

'We have to deal with the Cancer Tree once and for all, Dad,' said Jack, putting a bit more turkey on his plate. 'We made the humans so they could be our friends. While they remain cut off from us, there is a hole inside them that hurts them. Nothing will heal the deep sadness except our friendship. They'll never find true peace until they reconnect with us.'

The rest of the meal was eaten in silence. Godfrey served an amazing sherry trifle for afters. All three of them had second helpings. Afterwards they sat by the fire and watched the flames. Soon the darkness fell across the land.

'Well, Dad, this is it. Time to go.'

Godfrey screwed his face up. 'Really?'

'I've packed your suitcase,' said Sophia.

'Erm. Oh. Thanks. But I'm not taking anything,' said Jack.

Sophia and Godfrey looked at Jack.

'I'm leaving all my stuff here, I am only taking myself.'

'But you're going to be away for more than thirty years!' said Godfrey.

'Aye, and I shall live among the humans as one of them. This is going to be different from anything I've done before, Dad.'

At that moment, Godfrey knew that a new chapter of the world had begun. Jack was coming into his element.

The three figures hugged and said their farewells. Jack opened the door and saw the snow swirling in the darkness.

'I'm going in!' he said. He waved and walked into the night.

oOo

Maria Young was tidying up in the haberdashery shop, in Wigan, where she worked as an assistant. She was humming a tune and feeling very happy. As soon as her boss said she could go, Maria wasted no time.

'Have a good weekend!' said her boss.

'And you!' said Maria, as she left the shop.

She ran down the street as the snow fell on Wigan. She ran all the way to the lumberyard to meet the love of her life. And there he was – Joe Jones waiting at the gate for her. He loved her jet-black hair. She loved him for being tall and athletic. They embraced and kissed, then walked hand in hand to Maria's house, where Joe had been invited for tea.

Maria's mum had a lovely pile of sausage and mash ready when they arrived. The three of them sat round the table talking about their day as they ate.

Joe and Maria were soon to be married.

'Now, we've had a letter from the government,'

began Mrs Young. 'They're going to do a census and everyone has to go and register in the district they were born. '

'What?' said Maria.

'Bloomin' Italians!' said Joe.

Mrs Young handed her daughter the letter.

'This will cause chaos! You mean me and Joe have got to travel all the way back to Benchill in Manchester?'

'Looks that way, Love,' said Mrs Young.

'Fancy doing this now - in the wintertime. Why didn't they wait until summer?' said Maria.

'Bloomin' Italians,' muttered Joe again.

Later that evening, Maria walked Joe to the corner of the street where she kissed him good night.

Back at home, Maria helped her mum wash the dishes before they both turned in for the night. Content with her little life at the haberdashery shop, and the hunky Joe Jones, Maria drifted into sleep, dreaming of her wedding day.

oOo

'Hang on! Hang on!' shouted Gabriel to Eric. 'We'll have to land and look at the map! I can't see a thing in this blizzard!'

'Righto!' shouted Eric. 'Let's go for that park down there!'

The two angels landed in parkland and found an old bandstand where they took shelter.

Eric took the map out of his pocket and laid it on the floor. Gabriel knelt down beside Eric and they looked at the map together.

'Right, it looks like we are in the grounds of Haigh Hall,' said Gabriel, looking up to see if he could see the large house.

'And where is it we're looking for again?' said Eric.

'Coal Pit Lane in Bickershaw,' said Gabriel.

'Here we are!' said Eric. 'Bickershaw.'

'Coal Pit Lane is there,' said Gabriel. 'Number 134 Coal Pit Lane she lives at.'

'Right. Looks like we need to fly South East for a bit from here then,' said Eric, looking at his golden angel compass.

He folded up the map, and the pair flew off in the direction of Bickershaw in Wigan.

oOo

About half an hour later, Maria Young stirred in her sleep. It couldn't be morning already, she thought. But the room was getting brighter - very bright, in fact.

She sat up and to her horror saw a glowing figure standing at the foot of her bed.

'Ay up, young Maria. You have been chosen!'

Maria curled up at the far end of the bed.

'Don't be afraid, Love,' said the stranger. 'I am Gabriel, the servant of Godfrey, and I come with great news. This very night you shall conceive a child.'

'Think again!' said Maria, looking angry. 'I'm engaged to be married, so you can sling your hook, whoever you are!'

'No, no, Lass. It's nothing like that. This child will be the son of Godfrey. He is the one foretold in the ancient books. He has come to save his people.'

Although the situation was strange and terrifying, a sort of holy peace flowed from Gabriel into the room.

'But I have never slept with a man, so how would I become pregnant?'

'This very night, as you sleep, Sophia will visit you. You will not see her but she will place this gift of Godfrey in you. And when he is born, you should call the baby Jack. With Godfrey, anything is possible.'

'If this is true, if it is the promised visitation of Godfrey, then let it happen as you say.'

The vision began to dim; Gabriel smiled and was gone. Maria sat in the darkness wondering about what had just happened. Exhausted by the day's events she fell asleep with her head against the headboard and woke in the morning with a stiff neck.

When she told Joe what had happened in the night he didn't believe her at first and thought she had cheated on him. But the following night, Eric appeared to Joe, and convinced him that Maria was telling the truth.

The couple got married two weeks later and Miss Maria Young became Mrs Maria Jones. And just as Gabriel had told her, she found she was expecting a baby.

Shortly after their wedding day, Joe and Maria were summoned by the Italian rulers of Manchester to return to their place of birth to register in the census. Maria was not looking forward to the long journey, during her pregnancy. One weekend, Joe said he had a surprise for her; he had come home from work with a donkey and a rusty old coal cart.

'What is that contraption?'

'This, my dear, will be your transport to Benchill.'

'I'm not getting on that dirty old thing!'

'Ha ha. No, I am going to clean it up and everything. I got it cheap because it's rusty and the donkey is old. But I am going to do it up and make it beautiful - fit for a princess like you!

Maria was not convinced.

'You're going to make that old contraption fit for a Princess? Well I can't wait to see that!'

Joe worked on the contraption all weekend; cleaning, painting, repairing and polishing it. He even got a friend to groom the old donkey to tidy that up as well. By Sunday evening, Joe had made everything immaculate.

When Maria saw the transformation, she was very impressed.

'Wow! It's hard to believe that's the dirty contraption you brought home on Friday night.'

'Only the best for my girl.'

'It's immaculate!'

They loaded their things onto Maria's immaculate contraption and climbed aboard. Joe jerked the donkey's reigns and they were off, on the long journey to the place of their birth.

24

Eric goes on a mission

Godfrey was having a steaming bowl of porridge at the kitchen table in his tower. He looked out of the back window towards Mossley. He was lost in his thoughts when he heard a knock at the front door.

'Behold! I stand at the door and knock!' shouted a voice through the letter box. Godfrey heard laughter outside.

He opened the door to find Michael, Gabriel, and Eric laughing.

'Come in,' said Godfrey, smiling. 'I'll make a fresh brew.'

Soon the four friends were sitting by the fire drinking tea and eating angel cake.

'We thought we'd organise a welcome party for Jack,' said Michael.

'We've been rehearsing a big choir and everything,' said Gabriel.

Eric dunked his angel cake in his brew and listened carefully.

'We thought we could appear to the Italian King of Mancunia on the night Jack is born in human flesh to announce the arrival of the true king,' explained Michael.

'Oh I wouldn't do that,' said Godfrey, frowning. 'His heart is very dark. No, what I suggest is to announce the birth to a few simple folk– people whose hearts are not so hard and dark.'

'Oh. Good point,' said Michael.

Eric was looking longingly at the last slice of angel cake on the plate.

Michael nodded to Eric, who took the last slice with a smile. He was just about to take a bite when Godfrey announced, 'Now, young Eric. I have a special mission for you.'

Eric dropped his slice of angel cake into his brew as his mouth dropped open.

'Me Sir?'

'Yes. You Sir. It is top secret. You mustn't discuss it with anyone.'

Eric gulped.

'Eric, I want you to get down to the Irwell, very early tomorrow morning. I want you to bring me a small sample of the Cancer Tree – a little twig off it will do fine.'

'The Cancer Tree? Are you sure Sir?'

'Yes, very sure. I want you to put it in this glass jar and bring it straight back here. If at all possible, avoid being seen. Don't fly right into Manchester. That will alert the boggarts. Travel the last few miles over land. Top secret mission Eric!' Godfrey handed Eric a small jar with a screw top lid.

It had a label that read – CONTENTS HIGHLY TOXIC.

'This is a chance for promotion, young Eric!' said Michael.

Godfrey chatted to Michael and Gabriel for a few moments about the arrival of Jack in human form. Eric carefully tucked the special jar into one of his pockets. Then the three visitors took flight towards Manchester.

They touched down on Cringle Fields to visit Pat, the angel of Levenshulme. Pat had been expecting them, and had a rather yummy Lancashire Hotpot ready.

They all laughed and chatted over the meal. They loved hearing Pat's tales of recent events in Levenshulme. Pat had totally frustrated the plans of local boggarts looking to kill, steal and destroy at Crowcroft Park. There had been a major reduction in boggart victims in the area, and blessings were up by over thirty per cent.

Michael and Gabriel left after supper, but explained that Eric was on a top-secret mission for Godfrey and needed to stay the night. Pat sorted out the guest room, and Eric thanked her and bid farewell; he would be gone before first light. Eric set his golden angel alarm clock for three o'clock in the morning, and hoped he would not disturb Pat with his early start.

oOo

Joe and Maria arrived in Benchill as the sun was going down. Although they had the immaculate contraption, the road from Wigan was very rough in those days. Maria was already a few days overdue, so Joe was eager to find a place for the night.

The trouble was, neither of them had any surviving relatives in Benchill. Joe and Maria had only been born there as their parents had fled one of the Italian invasions of Manchester. As everyone else born there had also returned for the census, the few farmhouses and pubs were all fully occupied. They thought about sleeping under the immaculate contraption for the night, before Joe remembered Hollyhedge Farm. When he was growing up, he used to play on the fields there, and later had helped the farmer with the harvest to earn some pocket money.

Joe turned the donkey and the immaculate contraption in the direction of the Farm and hoped the farmer remembered him. It began snowing again as they bumped along an old track. Unfortunately, when Joe knocked on the door he discovered that the old farmer had long gone, and the new owner had a house full of census visitors already.

'But my wife is pregnant. She is due any day now,' pleaded Joe.

The farmer scratched his head.

'I'd love to help you young man but there is literally no more room.'

'But it's snowing and we have tried everywhere else.' said Joe.

'Well, the only thing I can suggest is sleeping in the barn for the night. At least you'll be warm and dry.'

Maria was holding her side wondering if the pain she felt was from the arduous journey from Wigan, or the onset of labour pains.

The farmer showed them to the barn. Joe got to work making a sort of inner shelter with the bales of hay – a hay bale inner sanctum, with a couple of bales to form a bed for them. The farmer brought them some blankets and some bread and hot soup. They settled for the night as the Northern winds whirled the snow out in the darkness across the fields.

'Bloomin' Italians,' muttered Joe again. 'Bloomin' census.'

They listened in the dark as the barn creaked and something howled in the distance. Eventually, exhausted from their long journey they both drifted into sleep.

oOo

As morning light painted the sky over Clayton Vale, a small figure draped in a dark cloak was quietly launching a coracle on the River Medlock. Eric reasoned that most days the Medlock flowed all the way down to the Irwell without anyone noticing it. If he flowed with it, perhaps no one would notice him.

---

coracle

- a small, round boat made of wickerwork covered with a watertight material, propelled with a paddle.

He pushed off from the bank and checked one last time that he had Godfrey's glass jar in his pocket. He didn't paddle too much, but just steered the little craft as the current took him downstream towards the mighty Irwell.

As it happened, he timed it just right. The boggarts had all gone to bed for the day after their night's work in the darkness. The humans, on the other hand, had not yet woken up.

As the Medlock surged into the Irwell, Eric steered closer to the bank so as not to be noticed. He passed by Manchester Cathedral. All was silent, apart from the sound of the running waters. He remembered with fondness that day– thousands of years back– when he had blown the trumpet to announce the arrival of Godfrey and Jack. He remembered Albert, the first man, being created on this riverbank.

Soon the great Willow Tree at Withy Grove caught his eye and he knew his target was just after that. He continued close to the bank, and caught hold of an overhanging branch to which he tied his coracle. He looked around. All was silent apart from the birds waking up in the tree tops. He walked down the bank and put his hand in his pocket to check he still had the little jar.

Still with its bright blue fruits, the Cancer Tree of old was before him. He put on some protective gloves, just to be on the safe side. He found his golden angel penknife and cut a small twig from the tree of death, which he placed in the jar. He screwed the lid back on tightly and looked intently at the dangerous sample.

So this little thing caused all this death, sickness and destruction, he thought. 'Very toxic indeed!' He put the jar and penknife away and walked back to his coracle.

To his surprise there was a stranger standing on the bank by the coracle. Eric realised he'd been caught by a boggart.

'And who might you be?' said the boggart.

'Me? Oh I'm no one. Just a simple traveller,' replied

Eric, wrapping the black cape around himself.

The boggart stepped right up to Eric and leaned close to his face. He sniffed Eric.

'Angel!' shouted the boggart. 'You're one of those angels that didn't join us in the rebellion!'

Eric really didn't want anyone shouting and drawing attention to his mission, especially a boggart. He drew his golden angel sword from its sheath, while the boggart drew his black sword. The boggart was much bigger than little Eric, but he fought as hard as he could.

Suddenly, the boggart pinned Eric to the ground.

'Tell me your business here, angel!' As they wrestled, the jar rolled out of Eric's pocket and plopped into the Irwell.

'So! That jar will tell me what you have been up to!' said the boggart.

The boggart changed his shape to that of a fish and leapt into the river.

Eric jumped into his coracle and paddled as fast as he could, flapping his wings a bit to catch up with the fish-shaped boggart and the jar, which was bobbing along the surface of the water. When Eric caught up with the boggart, it let out an ear-piercing shriek as Eric took his sword and sliced him in two. Both halves of the dead boggart floated on the surface of the Irwell, oozing with dark green boggart blood.

Eric caught up with the jar and scooped it up with his hand. He secured it in his pocket, and paddled away as fast as he could. Once he reached a quiet area he moored up to check he had the jar safe in his pocket and then took flight to Hartshead Pike to deliver his special cargo.

25

While shepherds washed their socks by night

Godfrey was out in the back garden chopping firewood when Eric landed. Snow lay all around but it had, at last, stopped. Godfrey rested on the axe for a moment as he watched his breath float into the cold morning air.

'Round the back, Lad!' he shouted to Eric, who was knocking on the front door.

Eric went round to the back of the tower and found Godfrey.

'I did it, Sir!' Eric held up the jar with the sample of the Cancer Tree.

'Oh, well done young Eric!' said Godfrey.

Eric told Godfrey about being caught by the boggart.

'Don't worry, Eric. At least you got away safely and secured the sample. No doubt there may have been another boggart or two hiding, so word could get back to Owd Hob. But he doesn't quite know what we are up to.'

'I'm not sure I do either,' said Eric.

'Best that as few folks as possible know what I'm up to at the moment,' said Godfrey, winking.

Eric helped Godfrey load two baskets of logs. They took them into the tower and lit a fire. Godfrey put the kettle on, and soon there was tea and toast on the table.

Eric was feeling a bit special. He was usually the assistant to Michael or Gabriel or one of the other senior angels. But here he was visiting Godfrey in his own right, after completing his first secret mission.

After breakfast, Godfrey took the glass jar that Eric had delivered, and locked it in a cupboard in his workshop, dropping the key back into his pocket.

'That'll keep me busy for a while,' said Godfrey.

'Well Sir, I best be getting over to Benchill for tonight's choir spectacular,' said Eric.

'Yes. Best you had. But before you go, there is another important matter to attend to.'

'Sir?' asked Eric.

Godfrey came over to Eric.

'Stand to attention, Lad.'

Eric stood to attention, expecting to be given another mission.

Godfrey took the little bronze pin from Eric's collar that read 'Junior Angel' and pulled a new pin from his pocket. It was a golden pin that read 'Angel First Class.'

Eric swelled with pride, still standing to attention.

'This day I appoint you to battle, Eric. Dark days are ahead of us. I need angels like you. And today I give you a new name. From this day, you shall be known as Eric Jedediah – meaning 'Beloved of God.' Well done soldier!'

When Eric left the tower for Benchill that morning, he barely needed wings to fly. He was so happy and excited with his promotion. He kept touching his gold pin to check it was still there. He couldn't stop smiling.

oOo

Out in the fields, beyond Baguley Hall in Wythenshawe, the snow was swirling in the moonlight. A flock of sheep were huddled together trying to keep warm. Down by the stream, two cloaked figures were having an argument about laundry.

'I cannot believe we are here washing your smelly socks, in the freezing cold, at this time of night!' said Jimmy.

'You were the one complaining about the smell!' replied Howard.

'Your feet stink!' said Jimmy. 'I can't sleep breathing that stench!'

'But I put clean socks on every morning,' said Howard.

'Yes, and by the end of the week your sandals don't fit. You are supposed to take yesterday's socks off before you put the clean ones on!' said Jimmy.

'It is far too cold for that! It is freezing out here at night, looking after these sheep. Layers, Jimmy, layers will keep your feet warm. I just layer up my socks,' said Howard.

'Just wash the blinkin' things and then let's go and find somewhere warm for the night,' said Jimmy.

As the pair argued by the stream, the dark night sky suddenly lit up brighter than midday. An angel appeared before them.

Howard dropped the pair of socks he was washing into the stream and they floated away into the night. Jimmy looked on open mouthed, as the glowing figure seemed to float above the waters. Howard thought he was about to wet himself.

'Do not be afraid!' said Eric – angel first class. 'I bring you good news. Right now in Benchill a baby is born. He is the promised saviour – Jack, the son of Godfrey. And this shall be the sign to you. You will find a baby wrapped in a blanket and laying in a rusty feeding trough in the old barn at Hollyhedge Farm.'

Jimmy was shaking so much he thought his legs would give way.

They thought the sky was bright while Eric was speaking, but suddenly the heavens lit up, and angels as far as the eye could see began to sing the most beautiful song. Such music had never been heard on Earth. There must have been a million angels there that night but in reality they were countless.

The two shepherds smiled.

They laughed.

They cried.

They shook.

They laughed.

They cried.

Then just as suddenly as the vision came, it was gone.

They looked to the dark sky. The moonlight was nothing compared to what they had just witnessed.

They looked at each other.

'Holy sheep poo!' said Jimmy.

'It was holy, but it certainly wasn't sheep poo!' said Howard.

'Where did he say?' asked Jimmy.

'Erm, Hollyhedge Farm,' said Howard. 'The old barn, I think.'

The two friends checked on the sheep. They were all huddled against a hedge and sleeping.

'Let's go!' said Jimmy.

'Flip!' said Howard.

When they reached Hollyhedge Farm, they found Joe Jones stirring a pan of soup over an open fire. They told him about the angels. Joe felt the hairs on the back of his neck stand up. He remembered his own angelic visitation nine months before.

He showed the two shepherds into the old barn, and there was Maria wrapped in a blanket. And, just as the angel Eric had told them, there was a little baby, wrapped in a blanket, sleeping in a rusty old feeding trough.

'What's that smell?' said Maria.

'Sorry! That is his smelly feet,' said Jimmy pointing to Howard.

Howard grinned apologetically.

Joe Jones brought the pan of soup in and shared it around with some bread as the two visitors told Maria about the angelic visitation. In fact, they told that story many times after that day, and news of the strange vision at Baguley spread across the whole of Manchester. Unfortunately, the story reached as far as Boggart Hole Clough in Blackley, and the ears of Owd Hob.

26

The child killer

The Red boggart of Lower Crumpsall was trying to drown a small child who had fallen into the River Irk when a Jack o' lantern found him. He told him he had been summoned to see Owd Hob, at Blackley, immediately. The Red boggart frowned and took his hand off the child's head. He followed the Jack o' lantern and set off towards Boggart Hole Clough.

The small child could not believe he had survived, as he climbed onto the riverbank. He had been sure he was about to die. He picked himself up and set off for home.

When the Red boggart reached Owd Hob's underground castle, the Jack o' lantern showed him down to the throne room.

'There you are! At last!' said Owd Hob. He motioned for the Red boggart to sit in a chair.

Owd Hob explained that Godfrey had somehow arranged for Jack to become a human, and that he had been born already.

'Now,' said Owd Hob, 'as you are in charge of killing small children in their infancy, I want you to track down this child and arrange an unfortunate accident.'

'But Master Hob, there are thousands of small children all across Manchester. How shall I find this particular one?'

'I don't care how you find him! I don't care what you have to do! All I care about is the death of Jack! This could be our greatest victory ever! This could bring me to full power! If we can destroy Jack, the apple of Godfrey's eye, we can break his heart forever!' yelled Owd Hob. 'Let me make myself perfectly clear, Red boggart. If you do not destroy Jack, I will destroy you!'

The Red boggart shook with fear.

'Yes, Master. Right away, Master.'

'Show him out!' said Owd Hob to the Jack o' lantern.

As the Red boggart walked back to Lower Crumpsall he pondered how he could ever find one particular boy child, from all the children in Manchester. Then he had a very dark thought.

'Kill them all!' he muttered to himself. The thought pleased him. He smiled. 'All I need is someone in power with a hard heart.'

oOo

The Emperor Lorenzo was standing at the upstairs window of Manchester Town Hall. He looked with pride across the city. Mancunia was far better since his people took over, he thought. Italian organisation. Italian taxes. Italian Roads. And soon the census would be completed, enabling them to tax more people.

Although Lorenzo was a young man to be Emperor

of Mancunia, he had achieved everything required of him. 'Excuse me your Majesty,' interrupted his secretary. 'Three important visitors have arrived from the East – the King of Northumbria has sent three ambassadors.'

'Oh? What do they want?' asked Lorenzo.

'Erm ... They are asking to see the new born king, Sir,' said the secretary.

'What?!' said Lorenzo, clearly disturbed. 'Show them in! I need to get to the bottom of this.'

Lorenzo knew that power could be gained and lost in a day. He had no children of his own, so he was curious as to who this newborn king could be.

He took lunch with the three visitors and questioned them about their search.

'It was when we saw a new star rise in the sky. We studied the ancient books and all our observations brought us to Mancunia, your Majesty,' said one of the ambassadors.

Lorenzo felt even more disturbed and sent for the temple manager of Manchester Cathedral to come at once.

The temple manager arrived within the hour, and listened carefully to the ambassadors' story.

'Well, your Majesty, there is probably nothing in it, but there is a prophecy in the ancient writings that says a future king of Mancunia will be born in Benchill,' said the temple manager.

'Benchill? Can anything good come from Benchill?' laughed Lorenzo.

After letting the temple manager go, Lorenzo addressed the ambassadors. 'I'll tell you what. You go and travel to Benchill. Search out this newborn king. Then come back here to the Town Hall and let me know where he is. I myself would like to visit and honour this future king.'

The ambassadors agreed and set off for Benchill.

Jimmy and Howard were moving their sheep towards Gatley when they saw two large carthorses pulling a grand coach along the lane. The driver was waving to them.

'That's a bit of a grand coach to be in Benchill,' said Jimmy. 'We better go and see what he wants.'

They whistled for the dogs to herd the sheep and keep them still. They reached the grand coach and horses, and met the ambassadors. As soon as they mentioned that they were looking for a special baby, the shepherds told them the story of the angelic visitation. The ambassadors were intrigued, and the shepherds gave them directions to Hollyhedge Farm.

By this time, Joe and Maria had moved into the guest room in the farmhouse, as the census was nearly complete and most of the visitors had returned back to their homes.

The grand coach pulled up at the farmhouse and the farmer came out to see what was happening.

'Oh you'll be looking for Joe and Maria Jones,' said the farmer.

He showed them in, and Joe and Maria were shocked to have such important visitors from so far away. The ambassadors presented expensive gifts for baby Jack and stayed the night at Hollyhedge Farm, sleeping in their grand coach.

During the night, one of the ambassadors had a dream, warning him about Emperor Lorenzo. Joe Jones also had a disturbing dream and told Maria that they needed to flee to Liverpool for a while.

By mid morning both parties were all packed up and ready to go. The farmer waved goodbye to his strange guests. The ambassadors' grand coach set off in one direction, secretly leaving Mancunia by a different route.

Joe and Maria climbed aboard the immaculate contraption and set off in the opposite direction for Liverpool.

When the Emperor Lorenzo realised that he had been tricked by the ambassadors he was furious. He paced up and down his office at Manchester Town Hall.

'How will I eliminate this threat to my throne now?' he asked himself.

Unseen, by his side, the Red boggart whispered in Lorenzo's ear.

'Kill them all ...'

'Yes! That's it!' said Lorenzo. 'I'll kill every baby boy in Benchill. No! Every baby boy in the whole of Wythenshawe! Yes!'

The following days were dark and bloody. All across Wythenshawe the massacre spread. Mothers and fathers wept over the bodies of their dead children. Southern Cemetery had to be extended to cope with all the new graves. Lorenzo knew his throne was secure for a while as the deep sadness increased across the land.

Ten years later, news came to Liverpool that Emperor Lorenzo had died from a strange illness and had been replaced by a new Italian Governor – Gnaeus Julius Agricola, known locally as Emperor Julius. Quietly and discretely, Joe and Maria brought young Jack back to Manchester. They settled in Newton Heath. Maria opened a little haberdashery shop on Oldham Road, and Joe built oak furniture in his workshop. Jack grew and became strong in spirit and filled with wisdom. And the grace of Godfrey was upon Him.

27

Godfrey invents the serum

Godfrey was working in his shed, behind Hartshead Pike. He lit a Bunsen burner just because he felt more like a scientist or inventor when that was burning. He had a test tube with a small sample of human blood. He pulled his goggles down and picked up his tweezers. He pulled a small splinter from the sample of the Cancer Tree branch that Eric had acquired for him and dropped it into the blood sample. Immediately, the solution turned jet black. He picked up a vial containing a sample of Jack's blood and extracted a small amount with a pipette, putting three drops into the black fluid. Then he added a few drops of the secret ingredient he had been working on.

He looked closely at the reaction. Yes! There it was. The fluid began to clear until, within a few moments, it was crystal clear.

'Eureka!' shouted Godfrey. If the human blood met the Cancer Tree sap, death came to the humans. But if Jack's pure blood and the secret formula were mixed into the equation, the Cancer Tree would die. The proportion required to kill the Cancer Tree would also kill Jack. But Godfrey had a plan to redeem that situation.

He scribbled down the exact quantities to recreate the solution, then turned off the Bunsen burner and went back to his tower.

'Wonderful!' he said to himself. 'I think I shall celebrate my discovery with a sausage and egg barm cake.'

barm cake

A North West version of a bread roll, sort of.

No sooner had the sausages begun to sizzle in the pan, when there was a knock at the door.

'Behold! We stand at the door and knock. If anyone hears our voice and opens the door ...,' shouted a voice through the letter box.

'Yes, yes. I know! You will come and eat with me,' said Godfrey, opening the door to Michael, Gabriel and Eric.

'Do you have to do that joke every time you call on me?'

'We think it's quite funny,' laughed Michael.

'Have you never heard of the rule of three?' asked Godfrey.

'Is the answer "The Trinity?"' asked Michael.

'No,' said Godfrey. 'It's the number of times you can repeat a joke before it becomes unfunny.'

Michael grinned.

'Oh something smells nice,' said Gabriel.

'I expect you'll all join me for a sausage and egg barm cake?' asked Godfrey, getting a few more barm cakes out of the bread bin.

'Oh yes please!' said Michael.

'I'll make us a brew,' said Gabriel.

Soon the four of them were sat round the table, eating sausage and egg barm cakes and drinking tea while listening to Godfrey tell of his discovery.

'So this serum can reverse the effect of the Cancer Tree on humans?' asked Michael.

'Well, it's not quite that simple. There is still a huge cost involved and a lot of work to do. But yes, this serum signals the end of Owd Hob's curse on the humans.'

'Yet again, Godfrey, you amaze us angels!' said Gabriel.

'Now I want to talk about rebuilding Jack's mansion at Brookdale,' said Godfrey. 'During the days of the locusts, the boggarts captured and demolished most of it. The Grey boggart lives in the ruins, but today I'm giving him a notice of eviction.'

He handed Eric an envelope.

'I think you know where to deliver this, young Eric Jedediah,' he said.

'Oh I'll deliver it. I'll deliver it right up his ...' began Eric.

'Yes! Thank you, Eric!' said Michael. 'Let us remember our manners.'

'Sorry, Sir,' said Eric. 'But them boggarts get right on my whatnots, they do.'

Michael and Gabriel stayed a while longer, as Godfrey explained how Jack's mansion would be restored to its former glory.

Eric Jedediah left to deliver the notice of eviction to the Grey boggart of Brookdale.

oOo

Eric landed at Brookdale. The narrow gate had been demolished in the uprising after the locusts. Not so much a narrow gate, but a broad way had been left in the boundary wall. Eric walked up the drive. The peacocks were long gone and the grounds that he had so carefully tended, with Philip, looked desolate. Rotting litter and dog poo was everywhere and the stench made him gag for breath.

Eric walked up to the ruins of the old mansion. He had so many fond memories of this place. But Godfrey no longer ran to greet visitors here. Jack's encouraging and life-giving presence was absent.

At the ruins, only the old dining room was still standing. Rubble and dirt lay all around.

A tear fell on Eric's cheek. Suddenly, there was the sound of music. Eric recognised the sound from summer days long passed, when all had been well with the world.

Then, suddenly, silence. The sky darkened.

'Ah, those were great days for you, weren't they?' said the Grey boggart, emerging from the rubble.

He came up to Eric and pushed his face very close.

'What do you want, Loser?' asked the boggart. His foul breath made Eric wince.

'You need to vacate this place,' said Eric.

'Never in a million years!' said the boggart.

'No. Not in a million years. But now,' said Eric, giving the boggart the envelope.

The boggart opened it and read the letter.

'Ha! Godfrey?' said the boggart. 'Is that the best you can do? Wake up angel-face! Owd Hob rules this land now. Come over to our side and stop wasting your time on futile resistance.'

'In the name of Godfrey, go or be destroyed you foul boggart!' said Eric. 'You no longer have authority to be here.'

The boggart laughed.

'Cancer Tree. Have you never heard of the Cancer Tree, junior angel?' mocked the boggart. 'Godfrey is powerless since we planted it.'

'Well, we will see about that. And that is Eric Jedediah to you!'

Eric took off. The boggart laughed as Eric left. Then the smile dropped from his face. The eviction letter was signed in blood.

oOo

Barry Malone lived in Littleborough. He was a human relative of Jack and passionate about calling people back to Godfrey.

Barry had gathered quite a following. His simple lifestyle and his call to people to respect each other had attracted many supporters. He spent his days near Hollingworth Lake. Many people travelled miles to see and hear this holy man. He called them to become clean and start a new life. He symbolised this by calling people to be dipped into the waters of the lake, as a sign that they were drowning their old life and starting a new one. Every day people queued up to be dipped in the waters.

Italian surveillance agents were observing him, as he had often spoken about the Emperor Julius' affairs with other women. This was very dangerous during the Italian occupation of Mancunia.

One Monday morning, Barry Malone was standing in Hollingworth Lake dipping people for a cleansed life. The queue was very long. He had just dipped a well-known prostitute into the waters, when she came up with a changed face.

'Wow! Oh wow! Oh wow!' she cried. 'I am free!'

She wrapped her arms around Barry and couldn't thank him enough.

'Every man I have ever known has abused me. But you, Barry Malone ...' her voice faded as she fought back the massive dam of tears.

'You, Barry Malone, are the first man who has ever told me the truth. You have not abused me. You have cleansed me and set me free today!'

'Aye. That's the love of Godfrey you have experienced, Lass,' said Barry.

The lady moved forward out of the waters of the lake, as Barry Malone looked for his next customer. He caught sight of the man wading into the lake and his mouth dropped open.

'No, no. no!' said Barry. 'Not you! I cannot dip you! You should dip me!'

Jack smiled and looked his cousin in the eye.

'Let's do it,' said Jack.

Barry Malone knelt down in the waters and bowed

his head to his cousin.

'I am not worthy to undo your sandals, Jack. I dip people in water. You will dip them in the life-force of Sophia,' said Barry.

Jack reached down to lift his cousin up. He embraced him.

'What did Godfrey call you to do?' asked Jack.

'He called me to dip people in the waters so they could know a better life,' said Barry.

'So dip me in the waters so we can all have a better life,' said Jack.

Reluctantly, Barry dipped Jack into the waters of the lake. As he came up, Jack punched the air.

'All systems go!' he shouted.

Jack and Barry embraced again. Barry was overwhelmed.

There was a loud noise from the sky. Everyone looked up. Some said it was thunder. Others said Godfrey had spoken and told them to listen to Jack.

Unseen by the crowd, Godfrey embraced Jack.

'I am well pleased, Lad!' said Godfrey.

Jack saw Sophia on the lakeside beckoning him. He followed her and she led him to Blackstone Edge – a lonely, desolate place. Soon Sophia disappeared. He learned how to survive in the wilderness. He sensed the time for his real work was just ahead. He found solitude and self-discipline on the hills of Blackstone Edge, to really attune to his humanity. He fasted and only drank water as he sought to connect with Godfrey. Remembering the abundance he'd enjoyed when he lived with Godfrey made Jack hungry. There are many large rocks at Blackstone Edge, even to this day. Jack sat on one of them and pondered the task ahead. He heard a loud roar and in the distance and saw a creature approaching. He remained still.

A large black lion was walking towards him - seeking someone to devour and looking Jack in the eye as it approached. Jack became alert and climbed off the boulder. He stood up straight, looking right back at the black lion.

The beast roared louder as it came near.

Jack noticed its teeth were broken and decayed. He stood his ground as the huge animal came right up to him, swishing its tail. Jack frowned at the smell of its vile breath as it let out a loud roar, right in his face.

'So we meet at last,' said the lion. 'If you really are the son of Godfrey, why do you sit here hungry? Use your magic and turn these stones into bread.'

'Humans don't just live by bread,' said Jack. 'They really begin to live when they connect with Godfrey.'

The lion walked up and down for a moment. 'You have come to save this world? I own this world. Become my servant, Jack, and all this world will be under your control.'

'This world belongs to Godfrey. You stole it from Albert and Edna but I am here to take it back!'

The lion laughed. 'And how do you propose to do that?'

'Well, let's see shall we?' Albert and Edna had everything they could ever want. They lived in great abundance. Yet they fell for your first temptation. I on the other hand am here in this remote area with nothing. Yet I shall not fall for any of your temptations. Everything I do in this human life will actually undo all the failings of the humans. I have come to set them free from your tyranny.'

The black lion leapt at Jack. But he found he had no claws to attack him.

The lion roared and paced but Jack was not intimidated by him. As his first tactic was instilling fear into victims, he was totally frustrated by Jack, who was not the least bit afraid of him. The lion left Jack and decided to wait for a better time to attack.

At the end of Jack's month on Blackstone Edge, he saw a figure approaching from the sky. Jack smiled with relief.

'It is finished!' said Eric, landing with supplies. 'Your challenge is finished!'

'Not really, Eric. It has only just started.'

'Steak and kidney pudding with chips and mushy peas, salt no vinegar?' Eric offered Jack a small parcel wrapped in newspaper.

'Oh Eric! You are a star!' said Jack. 'I could do with a drink though!'

'Ice-cold dandelion and burdock?' asked Eric, winking producing a chilled bottle.

'No wonder you were promoted!' laughed Jack. 'Attention to detail works every time!'

Jack enjoyed the infusion of steak and kidney pudding, chips and mushy peas, as never before. Tomorrow he was expected at the temple in Newton Heath.

28

The trainees

The next morning Jack arrived at the temple in Newton Heath. He had been invited to speak about his month of living in the wilderness. The temple manager handed Jack one of the books of the old prophecies that they were thinking about on that particular day.

Jack turned a few pages and read a short passage to those gathered.

The Spirit of Godfrey is upon me,
Because he sent me
To give the poor some good news;
He sent me to heal the broken-hearted,
To announce freedom to prisoners
And recovery of sight to the blind,
To set free those who are oppressed;
And to let the world know that Godfrey wants to do everyone a favour.

The crowd were familiar with these words of hope; that one day Godfrey would send a saviour to free them from the boggarts and, hopefully, the Italian occupation.

As Jack closed the book, everyone looked at him.

'This very day, the words of this ancient promise have come true before your eyes,' Jack began.

At first, the people were impressed with Jack's confidence and knowledge. But they soon realised he was claiming to be the one they had been waiting for, and began to murmur.

'Isn't this Joe and Maria's boy?' asked one.

'Didn't I buy some furniture off this lad not so long ago?' asked another.

Soon the temple manager was so irritated by Jack's claims, that he interrupted him. The crowd were getting angry and told Jack to leave. Before long they had ejected him from the temple.

As he left, two young men whose father owned the local fish and chip shop began following him and asking questions.

'We really liked what you were saying this morning,' Pete said.

'We'd really love to hear more.' said Jim.

'Well, Lads, I'm going to be on the road for a while now. If you want, you're welcome to join me,' said Jack. 'If you do, I'll give you bigger fish to fry.'

Pete and Jim collected a few things from home and told their father they were taking some time off to follow Jack. Their father wasn't very happy about it, but he wished them well.

Jack toured the area and the crowds grew. Day after day he visited new districts, and more and more people were impressed by him, especially when he started healing people.

Ian Travis had followed Jack's rise to fame with

great interest. He wondered if Jack would be the one to finally overthrow the Italian occupation of Mancunia. Ian was an activist. He had worked with others to stir up trouble for the Italians and thought that if a few people worked together, they could destabilise Italian power. As Jack became ever more controversial, Ian asked if he could join Jack's trainees.

Soon Ian took on the role of treasurer, for the funds people gave to Jack and his team, but unknown to them Ian began taking money for himself.

Down at Miles Platting, old Bart, the blind beggar, sat on the corner with his cap held out for money from passers-by. As the crowds followed Jack towards the city centre, Bart heard the commotion and asked what all the fuss was about.

'It's that bloke Jack, everyone's been talking about,' said a bystander. 'The one who heals people and gives them hope.'

'Jack! Jack! Help me!' yelled old Bart.

'Be quiet old man!' said people in the crowd. 'He's not interested in you.'

But old Bart yelled louder.

Jack stopped when he heard old Bart shouting above the crowd.

'Bring that old man to me,' said Jack.

A couple of women led the blind man to Jack as people in the crowd tut-tutted about the old beggar's interruption.

'What do you want from me?' asked Jack.

'I want to see again,' said old Bart.

Jack placed his hand over old Bart's eyes and

became still for a moment, then said 'Be open!'

He took his hand off old Bart's face and the old man smiled. Then he began to laugh. And then he cried.

'I can see! I can see you! And you! And you!' he said, pointing to different people in the crowd.

Everyone was amazed and cheered.

One day, Jack walked to Crime Lake with his little group of followers. As they walked along the bank of the lake they met a man fishing.

'Caught anything?' asked Jack.

'Not really,' said the fisherman.

'How would you like to fish in a bigger lake with loads of fish?' asked Jack.

'How far would I have to go?' asked the man, looking at Jack. 'Hey! Aren't you that bloke I keep hearing about? The one wot heals people and tells stories?'

'I am,' said Jack.

The man jumped up and shook his hand.

'Pleased to meet you! I am John. Someone should write down stories of all that you are doing and make a book of them!'

'Well, who would want to do that?' asked Jack.

'Well I would for one!' said John.

'Righto, well why don't you join our little community and you can make notes for your book as we go along?' said Jack.

John agreed and packed up his fishing tackle.

Before long, Jack had twelve men and eight women who travelled everywhere with him. Some days he took this little group of trainees to a secluded place and taught them how to heal sickness by the power of Godfrey. Other days they were busy, as Jack taught large crowds in Platt Fields. As the sun went down, people would bring their sick friends and relatives to Jack, and he healed them all.

One Sunday, Jack went to the temple at Manchester, on the banks of the Irwell. As he entered the great cathedral, built by Simon Fairhurst, a man with severe arthritis in his right hand approached him.

'Oh Jack! If that really is you, please take my pain away!' said the old man.

The temple managers heard the man calling to Jack. They disliked this new idea of speaking in the open air and healing the sick. People were leaving the temples to seek out Jack wherever he was speaking to the crowds. The temple mangers were losing money, as people weren't there when the collection was taken. They didn't like Jack. They didn't like him at all.

The senior temple manager came over to Jack and the man with the arthritic hand.

'Now we don't want your circus antics here young man,' said the temple manager.

Jack looked at the temple managers.

'You dress in strange robes, wear strange pointy hats, you perform for the crowds twice daily. Your presentations are musicals punctuated with songs and solo performances. Yet here is this old man with a very painful hand and you don't want me to heal him? If you clowns want to close down the real circus, I'd start by looking in the mirror,' said Jack.

'How dare you speak to us like that!' said the temple manager. 'We are the custodians of Martin Simmonite's piano! We expound and teach people the ten laws inscribed on that sacred piano. And you have the temerity to speak to us in this insulting way?'

Jack turned to the old man.

'Stretch out your hand,' said Jack.

The man did as he was told, and as Jack touched the man's hand all the pain drained away and his fingers opened fully for the first time in years.

'Thank you! Thank you, Jack!' said the man.

The people all saw the miraculous healing and were amazed.

But the temple managers were seething as they ejected Jack and the healed man from the building. They proposed a meeting to discuss how to kerb Jack's influence on the people of Manchester.

Pete, Jim, John, and Jack's other trainees were all there to witness this. The group walked down the banks of the Irwell until they came to Angel Meadow where a crowd had gathered.

'Tell us about the kingdom of Godfrey!' shouted a lady in the crowd.

The people sat on the grass and Jack began to tell them stories of the hidden kingdom.

'Godfrey is always close to you. He is nearer to you than your hands and feet. Closer to you than your own breath,' began Jack.

Unlike the temple managers, Jack talked to people about things they were interested in.

He talked about fishing and building.

He talked about marriage and divorce.

He talked about animals and business.

He talked about jewellery and investments.

He talked about baking and parties.

He talked about eating and drinking.

He talked about friends and neighbours.

He talked about love and hate.

He talked about fathers and sons.

He talked about mothers and daughters.

He talked about forgiveness and reconciliation.

He talked about working and resting.

The more Jack talked to ordinary people, the more they gathered around him. And the more they gathered around him, the more jealous the temple managers were.

oOo

Down in the underground castle at Boggart Hole Clough, every boggart and Jack o' lantern had gathered at Owd Hob's command. He gathered the troops because his tactics were not working.

'This son of Godfrey is a menace!' declared Owd Hob, gesticulating wildly. 'Everywhere we have established sickness and disease, Jack is spreading healing and life! Where we have spread hatred, he is bringing reconciliation. But yesterday was the last straw! Yesterday this irritating man actually went into Moston Cemetery and opened up a grave of a man who had been dead for four days. Then he brought him back to life!

I say, enough is enough!

Death is our most powerful weapon. We cannot have anyone undoing death!

So from this hour, I charge every one of you here

with a single task. We must work as one and kill Jack. Death must come to the life-giver whatever the cost!'

They all cheered for Owd Hob and committed themselves to the task, though most of them did it out of fear of what Owd Hob would do to them if they didn't comply.

'Death to Jack! Death to Jack!' they shouted together.

The red boggart, who had failed to kill Jack in his infancy, sat at the back, trying not be seen by Owd Hob. He feared being singled out for punishment.

After the boggarts and other creatures of darkness had all gone home, Jinny, Owd Hob's wife, made a suggestion.

'The answer may lie with the Emperor Julius,' she said.

'What do you mean?' asked Owd Hob.

'Well, the Italians care little for the lives of these people,' said Jinny. 'Their punishments are severe and their executions are barbaric. If one of our number could arrange for Jack to be arrested for something, we could possibly stir things up so he gets the death penalty.'

Owd Hob stroked his chin. 'Hmm. You may be onto something there my dear,' he said. 'The Italian death penalty ...'

oOo

Barry Malone had a queue of people wanting to drown their past. He was standing waist deep in Hollingworth Lake, dipping the penitents into the water. Every two hours, he gave a short talk about doing the right thing in life.

On this particular day, he launched into the folly of ruining your marriage. He used the current Emperor Julius as an example. He listed five particular points of the Emperor's affair with the other woman.

He was in full flow when two tall, dark-haired Italian surveillance men stepped out of the crowd, dragged him out of the lake and wrestled him to the ground. He was handcuffed, and before the crowd could react he was whisked away. He was never seen in public again.

The Italian authorities threw Barry Malone into Strangeways Jail. He refused to moderate his messages so they put him in solitary confinement.

Emperor Julius was holding a birthday party for Gail, the daughter of his mistress. She was twenty-one-years-old. Manchester Town Hall was throbbing with music and lights.

Gail signalled to the emcee and he switched the music to something quite raunchy. Gail took centre stage and performed a dance so erotic that every male in the building stood open mouthed. The crowd went wild.

Emperor Julius was amazed. He thought this girl's mother was passionate but now the daughter had put all sorts of thoughts into his head. Overcome with emotion he congratulated the young dancer.

'Gail my dear! That was amazing! Right now, before all my guests, I promise to give you anything you want, up to half of Mancunia!' promised Julius.

All the guests gasped.

Gail was unsure what to ask for. She looked to her controlling mother, who had suggested this dance in the first place. Her mother came over and took her arm. She pulled her to one side, smiling and waving to the crowd.

'What shall I ask for, Mum?' said the girl.

'This is our chance!' said her mother. 'If we can eliminate Barry Malone, Julius will marry me and we will be rich!'

'What?' said Gail.

'Ask for Barry Malone's head on a plate. Here. Now. In front of everyone!' said her mother.

Gail was disturbed but, as usual, her controlling mother got her own way. Emperor Julius was also very disturbed. He hated Barry Malone's comments as much as his mistress but this seemed to going too far.

His mistress seized the opportunity and demanded Julius deliver on his promise. The party continued with music, chatter and drunkenness. Soon the head waiter came into the room with a silver tray. And there on the tray was the decapitated head of Barry Malone. The blood oozed from the head on to the tray. Gail's mother made Gail accept the gift.

Soon after, most guests made their excuses and left. They were used to Italian barbarism but only at public executions and behind closed doors. This "present" to the daughter of his mistress had shocked even his most loyal friends and supporters.

When Barry Malone's friends heard of his demise, the deep sadness fell upon the land once more.

29

Jack gets angry

Eric was on a familiar flight path. The Manchester mist and drizzle was not helping navigation. Eric was experiencing both emotional and meteorological turbulence; human brutality disturbed him. But Eric could do this flight with his eyes closed: head for Duckinfield and then glide on the Southerly wind toward Mossley, and begin the descent.

He arrived at Hartshead Pike in the early evening, landing a few yards short of the tower. This was not a day to shout jokes through Godfrey's letterbox. He reached the front door and looked back towards Manchester. Sadness filled his heart. He swallowed hard and knocked on the door. Godfrey seemed unsurprised to see his angel friend.

'Eric, I thought you would come some day soon,' said Godfrey.

Eric gulped with fear. He went into the tower and stood by the fire.

'Sir, they have beheaded Barry Malone,' said Eric.

Godfrey froze. He stepped outside for a moment and

quietly wept in the rain. 'They chopped off his head?' he whispered in dismay.

Eric looked at the figure on the hillside. The person he most respected was devastated. Eric was unsure what to do.

Godfrey knew it was time. It was the moment he had wanted to avoid ever since he created humans. He walked back indoors.

'Eric, get back down to Manchester. Tell Michael to put every angel on maximum alert. Tell Gabriel to take a legion of angels and shadow Jack. If he calls, they must act swiftly.'

'Sir, will the kingdom stand?' asked Eric.

'That all depends on Jack. That is why I need full security around him this weekend. If he falls, we all fall!'

Eric saluted Godfrey.

'Sir, whatever happens, you can count on me!'

'You know the enemy, Eric. They are ruthless. But now, hurry Lad. Go and tell Michael and Gabriel the new orders.'

Eric took off into the wind and rain, and headed towards Manchester.

Alone in his tower, Godfrey wept again. He loved Jack more than anything. The thought of what was about to happen tortured his soul. But as always, he realised he had things he must do if the humans were to survive Owd Hob's assault.

He packed the vial of the secret serum he had made some years before, along with a golden syringe and a few supplies and brought the tandem round to the front of the tower. The sun was setting. He looked towards

Manchester and sang the secret song that called to Sophia. He felt the weight of the whole human world on his shoulders as he set off into the night, down Lily Lane, heading for Gorton.

oOo

The blue boggart slithered down the deep damp hole at Boggart Hole Clough. The Jack o' lantern guards greeted him and led him to the bowels of the castle to meet with Owd Hob.

'I hope you bring me good news blue boggart.'

'I believe I do, your Royal Ugliness. I have planted a devious plot in the heart of one of Jack's trainees. This very night he will do a deal with the temple managers and help them get Jack arrested for treason.'

'Treason? I don't see how you will make that charge stick, but if you do, there is a promotion for you. You will be aware that the Italian penalty for treason is torture, followed by being nailed to a tree and allowed to die slowly as the blood drains from the body.'

'I am indeed, Master. And that is my hope and intention.'

'Wonderful!' said Owd Hob. 'I shall travel into the city to watch this spectacle. Soon, full power will be mine, and then we shall eliminate every last soul who is open to Godfrey. We shall wipe out his precious son, his precious followers and turn the hearts of those who remain to join us in the darkness. Then we shall laugh as Godfrey's heart and kingdom is finally broken.'

oOo

Jack and the trainees were having a picnic half way up Tandle Hill near Oldham. When they had finished eating, Jack asked Pete, Jim and John to climb to the top of the hill with him while the others rested.

At the top of Tandle Hill a strange thing happened. Jack began to glow. He got brighter, and brighter, until he was brighter than the sun. The four friends squinted to see two other figures talking to Jack about the coming weekend. Somehow they knew one of figures was Martin Simmonite.

Then they heard a voice.

'This is my son. Listen to him.' They looked on in awe, each hearing the voice of Godfrey.

'Let's build a monument to this!' said Pete. He didn't know what he was talking about.

The two visitors disappeared and Jack returned to normal.

Jack put his hand on Pete's shoulder and smiled.

'This is about a man, a message and a movement, Pete. The day it becomes a monument it will die,' said Jack.

The four of them went down the hill to find the others.

'It is time,' Jack told them. 'We must walk into Manchester for the special weekend.'

As Jack's little group walked towards Manchester, people began to join them, and before long the walk had turned into a procession. Along the way a man insisted that Jack should use his donkey as transport, and Jack accepted.

As people lined the streets and watched the procession they believed that Jack could set them free from the Italian occupation. They began to pull little bits of privet out of the hedges and lay them on the ground before Jack's donkey, as a sign of good luck.

'Long live King Jack!' the people shouted. 'We want freedom! Set us free Jack!' On and on the crowd cheered, feeling that their saviour had finally come.

The procession arrived at Manchester Cathedral and the crowds gathered for the first of many services for the special weekend.

As Jack walked around the great temple he noticed all sorts of stalls and tables selling things. He watched as people were charged an entrance fee on this holiday weekend. And the more he watched, the more he became angry.

'This was supposed to be a house of prayer to Godfrey!' he shouted. He looked at the temple managers who were watching him closely.

'But you have turned it into a den of thieves and robbers!' Jack walked up to one of the stalls and turned it over, scattering the merchandise across the floor. Everyone gasped.

Again and again he turned over the tables of the stallholders.

The temple managers called the temple guards and had Jack and the trainees thrown out.

'This is the last straw!' said the senior temple manager. 'This madman must face justice!'

Jack and the trainees left the city centre and headed out towards Gorton.

The temple managers went to the Town Hall and asked for an audience with Emperor Julius. When they told the officers of the emperor that they had evidence of a possible act of treason, the Emperor saw them at once. He listened to their story but the evidence seemed a bit flimsy.

'You know, we Italians tolerate you local people,' said Julius. 'You have strange ways that we have no interest in. However, peace is more profitable than war. And so we compromise with you. Rest assured, if you people ever step over the line of usefulness, you will be eradicated. I think this man you are concerned about is just one of your many mad preachers. They come and go.'

He looked at the temple managers and saw that they understood his reference to Barry Malone.

'However, I cannot ignore his huge following. Everyone is here for your special holiday and I don't want trouble. I will give you a warrant for his arrest but I don't want any drama in my city this weekend. The place is packed with your people celebrating. If you can detain this man discretely, I will cross-examine him myself.

The temple managers took the warrant and went away to discuss how they could find Jack and arrest him.

30

Breaking bread

Manchester was in party mood. It was the long weekend holiday of Brickster. The people of Manchester celebrated the story of Martin Simmonite rescuing his people from slavery in Briscoe Lane Brickworks.

Every home had a brick in the window, decorated with candles and oil lamps. Children were given chocolate bricks as a treat. People wore daffodils on their lapel as a sign of new hope. But above all else, friends and families came together to celebrate over a roast beef dinner with all the trimmings, and the wine flowed freely all weekend.

Jack and his trainees booked the upstairs function room at a little cottage pub in a vale in Gorton. On Thursday evening they gathered for a celebration supper. Soon all twelve men and eight women had arrived and the drinks were flowing. A table had been set and the little gang sat down and shared stories of healings and lives transformed as they had taught people about the love of Godfrey.

Soon the food arrived and there was an abundance of everything. Jack remembered the days of abundance at Brookdale, which far exceeded even this wonderful feast before him.

Ian, the crooked treasurer, sat opposite Jack and was on second helpings before everyone else. The waitress refreshed the bread rolls and opened another bottle of red wine.

'My friends,' said Jack. 'This weekend will change the world forever. Dark times are ahead for each one of us.'

The trainees didn't know what Jack meant.

'I no longer call you trainees, but friends. This is what will happen this weekend.'

Jack took a large bread roll and held it up for all to see.

'This is my body,' he said. And then he ripped the bread into small pieces and gave a bit to each of them.

The idea of Jack being ripped to pieces disturbed them, but sometimes Jack was a bit profound so they ate the bread quietly.

Jack took the fresh bottle of red wine and held it up before them.

'You see this? This is my blood - which is given for you.'

He slowly trickled the wine from the bottle into a large glass. Again the group were troubled at the thought of Jack bleeding to death, but they quietly took turns and shared the glass round, each having a sip as Jack had indicated.

Slowly the conversation resumed as they each murmured about what Jack had just done.

Ian went to take another bread roll but Jack put his hand on Ian's hand. Ian looked at Jack, who looked him in the eye.

'What you are going to do, do it quickly,' said Jack.

Ian blushed and didn't know what to do. Jack held his gaze. Ian got up from the table and went out into the darkness. It was night. The others thought Jack had sent him on an errand of mercy.

After Ian left, Jack paid the bill and gathered his friends.

'We need to go and seek Godfrey now,' said Jack.

His followers knew he had tried to tell them something with the bread and wine thing, but they were unsure what was happening. Jack led them on a short walk through the night to the garden of Gorton Cemetery.

'Sit here while we pray,' he told his followers. He took Pete, Jim and John a little further into the garden.

'My soul is very troubled. Death is in the air,' he said to his three close friends. 'Stay here and pray to Godfrey.'

He walked a little further and began to pray.

Godfrey appeared to Jack as he prayed.

'Dad! If it is possible, please take this task away from me,' said Jack. 'The evil here is too deep.'

Godfrey wept.

'But if I am the only one who can do this, then I am willing,' said Jack.

Unseen by any human, Godfrey embraced Jack as he wept.

Jack went back to his closest friends and found them sleeping.

'Hey! Just one hour is all I am asking!' said Jack.

Pete, Jim and John woke up and promised to pray.

Jack went back and spoke to Godfrey.

'This is going to be hell,' said Godfrey.

'I know,' said Jack. 'But this is the reason I became human.'

'We have never been separated before Jack,' said Godfrey. 'I dread to think of that hour.'

'Dad, we have to deal with the Cancer Tree once and for all,' said Jack. 'Let's get this over with.'

Jack went back and again found Pete, Jim and John snoring on the grass. The full meal and several glasses of wine had taken their toll.

'Wake up!' he said. 'My betrayer approaches!'

The three men rubbed their eyes and apologised as they saw Ian approaching.

Ian led a delegation of temple managers and Italian policemen, who were carrying blue lanterns.

Ian stepped forward and hugged Jack.

'You betray me with an embrace?' asked Jack.

Ian avoided eye contact and didn't speak. He'd told the police that the one he embraced would be the man they were looking for.

'Are you Jack of Newton Heath!' shouted one of the policemen.

'I am,' said Jack.

The temple managers and all the policemen fell to the ground, overwhelmed by Jack's authority. He feared no one. He had done nothing wrong.

'Have you come to arrest me with swords, spears and clubs like a violent criminal,' asked Jack. 'I spoke publicly in your parks and temples in Mancunia, and you never arrested me. But now the true darkness has come, this is your hour.'

When Jack's friends saw what was happening to him, they all abandoned him and ran away into the night.

Jack was arrested and taken into custody.

Unseen by human eyes, a legion of angels drew their golden swords, waiting for Jack's command. But Jack remained silent.

One of the temple managers gave Ian a small bag containing thirty gold coins.

Down at Strangeways prison, Jack was interrogated. First the temple guards questioned him. They had finally got their nemesis behind closed doors. The senior temple manager came to Jack, who was handcuffed.

'So you are here to rescue people?' he said. He spat on Jack's face.

'You are a stupid madman,' said the temple manager.

Jack didn't answer.

The senior temple manager motioned to his personal guard.

'Please explain to Jack the correct procedure of respect for the temple,' said the manager.

The guard stepped forward and smiled at Jack. Then he punched him so hard in the stomach that Jack collapsed on the floor.

Before he could get his breath the guard kicked him in the face and then stamped on his head.

He then pulled him up by his hair and kicked him

hard in the groin before throwing him to the ground.

The senior temple manager bent down to the ground. 'Are you really the son of Godfrey, the saviour we are waiting for?' he asked.

'I am,' said Jack.

'What further need do we have of witnesses? You have heard the blasphemy! What do you think?' said the temple manager.

They all condemned him and said he deserved the death penalty. Then other guards began to spit on him, and to blindfold him, and to beat him.

And the Italian police officers struck him, punched him and humiliated him.

One of them brought a strip of purple material and wrapped it round Jack.

'Here is a robe for the great king!' he mocked.

Another police officer found some Pyracantha stems with long, sharp thorns. He twisted them into a vicious circle. 'Here is your crown O king!'

He pressed the sharp thorny crown into Jack's head.

Blood streamed down Jack's face. The pain was excruciating.

Unseen by the human tormentors, Owd Hob stood in the corner of the cell laughing.

When they tired of tormenting Jack for the night, his abusers threw him to the ground and left him in the darkness of solitary confinement in Strangeways Jail.

At six o'clock next morning, Italian guards came into the cell.

Jack was taken to a courtroom at Manchester Town Hall and hauled before Emperor Julius.

Julius listened to the temple manager's charge of treason.

He looked at the dishevelled little man that was Jack. His eyes were swollen and bruised. His hair was matted with dry blood from the crown of thorns. His clothes were covered in bloodstains.

'Ha! So you are the new king I am supposed to be afraid of?' said Julius. 'You are nothing – a nobody!'

Julius looked at the temple managers.

'He definitely claimed to be a king, your Highness!' said the senior temple manager.

Julius grabbed Jack's hair and pulled his head up.

'So you are a king then?' he asked.

'I am,' said Jack.

Julius laughed. He motioned for Jack to be put back in the cells, ready for execution later that day. By Italian law, at that time, anyone sentenced to death for treason could be freely tortured by Italian soldiers.

At Strangeways Jail, the soldiers had a bet on how hard they could whip a prisoner without him dying. They had plenty of experience, and some prisoners had died before their execution due to the brutality of the soldiers. The Emperor was not very bothered by this as long as fear ruled the day.

Jack was tied to a post, and they took turns whipping him to as near death as possible as they laughed. Before midday arrived, Jack's back was like a raw hamburger.

Eventually the temple managers arrived. Even they were shocked by Jack's brutal treatment.

They dragged him from Stangeways Jail down towards Deansgate. As they passed the Cathedral, Jack looked up and saw all the temple staff on the steps.

They seemed to be shocked by his appearance but no one spoke in his defence.

They passed the great Willow Tree at Withy Grove and Jack remembered the day Godfrey created humans by drawing a line round him on the banks of the Irwell.

He was dragged a short way to where the Cancer Tree stood.

Unseen by the humans, a legion of angels drew their swords. On the opposite bank of the Irwell, a legion of boggarts drew theirs.

'Nail the idiot king to that tree!' shouted the Italian commander in charge of executions.

The soldiers stripped Jack of his clothes and lifted his wounded body. They wrapped his arms and legs around the Cancer Tree and tied him to the tree with ropes.

'Let the people of Mancunia beware!' shouted the commander. 'This is what happens when you attempt to overthrow the Emperor of Mancunia!'

Jack was nailed by his hands and feet as he was forced to hug the Cancer Tree.

A crowd gathered and all gasped at the Italian brutality.

One man shouted, 'If you are the son of Godfrey, come down off the tree! Save yourself and us!'

Unseen by the crowd, Godfrey stood by the Cancer Tree weeping.

Jack was struggling to cope with the physical human pain of it all when something much worse happened. Where the nails had been driven through his hands and feet, his blood began to mingle with the poisonous sap of the Cancer Tree.

The dark poison infected Jack's blood and he felt the light of life drain from his body. For the first time in his existence, Jack could neither see nor hear Godfrey or Sophia.

As Jack began to die, Godfrey climbed the Cancer Tree. Human eyes could not see him and that was the problem he had come to remedy.

He took the syringe loaded with the secret serum and injected it into Jack's body. Slowly the chemical reaction took effect.

'Dad! Dad! Why have you abandoned me?!' cried Jack from the tree.

Godfrey was fighting back tears. 'I will never leave you or forsake you, Jack. You cannot see or hear me now because of the Cancer Tree. This is how humans live. But soon all that will change.'

The sap of the Cancer Tree was deadly. But the serum was also deadly.

A short distance away, sitting under a tree, Sophia was weeping. This was the vision she had seen when Albert, the first man, had been created.

Back in the crowd stood Jack's mum, Maria, and his close friend John.

When Jack was born, the angelic choir had lit the night sky. But now he was dying, there was only darkness. At three o'clock it started to rain and most people headed for home. They all assumed it was over for Jack.

The poison of the Cancer Tree was indeed killing Jack. But as the poison met the serum it began to destroy the poison of the Cancer Tree, just like

Godfrey's experiments up at Hartshead Pike. By midnight the Cancer Tree was dry, withered and dead. All its power and poison had gone. The effect of the serum mingling with Jack's blood had spread down through the tree's vast root system and had killed every last part of it.

When the Italian soldier was sure that Jack was dead, he ordered his body to be removed from the Cancer Tree and released to Jack's friends.

They wrapped his body in a shroud and took him to Southern Cemetery. A rich man called Jacob of Altrincham offered the use of his family mausoleum. The Italian authorities only allowed this on condition that they could seal the mausoleum with a very large stone. The Emperor wanted to be sure that Jack's influence on the people of Mancunia was definitely over.

They laid Jack's body in the tomb. As it was late at night, the soldiers hurried his friends out of the tomb and sealed it with the huge stone. They cemented it in place. Jack's friends stayed the night in Whalley Range, with a friend of Maria. They didn't really sleep that night as they relived the horror of seeing Jack executed.

It began to rain again. All through that dark night, the little back streets of Manchester were cloaked in fine drizzle.

oOo

Down at Boggart Hole Clough, Owd Hob's underground Castle was in full party mode. Every boggart and Jack o' lantern was celebrating the death of Jack and Godfrey's broken heart. Owd Hob congratulated various boggarts who had been instrumental in killing Jack. The party went on all weekend.

In the dead of night, Owd Hob climbed onto the platform and addressed his troops.

'My fellow boggarts and agents of darkness, changes of government have occurred frequently in history, and in the history of humans. It is certain, however, that never was a change of government attended with such far-reaching consequences as the change that happened this Friday.

Thanks to the hard work, craftiness and deception of everyone here, our new government has left behind an icy stream of blood and tears in the path of its creation. And for that I thank you.

Godfrey had continually plotted against our boggart kingdom. He was hostile and aggressive to boggarts at every opportunity, until our glorious war broke out. Perhaps now Godfrey will regret being so hostile to us and underestimating our determination to win.

Jack is dead. Godfrey is powerless. The kingdom is ours!'

'Long live Hob! Long live Hob!' his audience cheered. They toasted Owd Hob, as the celebration continued.

31

The incident at Southern Cemetery

That Saturday, the whole of Manchester was silent. Families were at home to celebrate Brickster weekend. But no one went out. It was like the stillness of Christmas Day but without the happiness. The deep sadness seemed to be in everyone's heart, including the Italians.

Those who had been healed or helped by Jack sat by their windows and stared out at the rain. The people of Manchester had hoped Jack was going to free them from the Italian occupation. But now he was dead.

The Manchester drizzle continued all day long, as though even the angels were weeping.

oOo

As daybreak on Sunday painted silver linings on the dark clouds, the constant driving rain continued to make puddles everywhere. The whole of Manchester was still asleep. Down in Southern Cemetery two figures wearing yellow raincoats and yellow Wellingtons had landed in a puddle.

'Now where is this grave?' asked Gabriel.

'Hang on a minute!' said Eric, putting up his yellow angel umbrella. He pulled out a hand-drawn diagram that Godfrey had given him the previous night.

'He said it was one of them posh graves – a mausoleum – so it should be easy to find,' said Eric.

They followed Godfrey's diagram and located Jack's tomb.

Angels in bright raincoats rolled the stone away.

Then they stood guard. A few moments later Godfrey arrived on his tandem. He wiped the raindrops from his face and, turning to look into the distance, began to sing the song of creation.

Soon the rain stopped. Godfrey and the angels waited. The wind began to pick up and before long Sophia appeared.

Eric and Gabriel stood either side of the entrance to the tomb, and Godfrey and Sophia went in.

In the shadows of the mausoleum Godfrey could see the corpse of his son, lying in the blood-stained shroud. The body had been wrapped in black chains, which were held at the ends by a tall, dark hooded figure standing in the corner of the tomb. His face was not visible but Godfrey was familiar with the creature – it was Death.

'You cannot keep him,' said Godfrey.

Death hissed. 'All human flesh belongs to me in the end.'

'You forget the ancient law,' said Godfrey.

Death hissed again.

'What ancient law?' Death was irritated that anyone would question his power.

'No pure and innocent human can be held by you for more than three days,' said Godfrey.

Death pulled the chains tighter.

Sophia stepped forward and knelt by Jack's body. She pulled back the shroud from Jack's face. As she kissed him, Death let out a shriek. His hooded gown fell to the floor and he was gone. The black chains fell from Jack's body.

Jack opened his eyes and looked at Sophia.

'Is it finished?' he asked, exhausted.

'It is finished!' said Sophia.

Godfrey took out a set of clean clothes from his backpack and laid them out for Jack. Godfrey and Sophia left the tomb while Jack got dressed. Soon Jack walked out into the morning light.

Eric and Gabriel stood to attention.

'Good to have you back, Sir!' said Gabriel.

Jack embraced the two angels. 'Good to be back!'

'Righto, Jack, we should get to our next appointment,' said Godfrey.

'Aye. I'm looking forward to this,' said Jack.

'Eric, you stay on duty here for the humans,' said Godfrey. 'Gabriel, you go ahead and gather the troops at Blackley.'

Sophia had already disappeared.

Gabriel took off into the morning sky. Godfrey and Jack climbed on the tandem and cycled off.

Eric, sat on the large stone by the empty tomb. He took out his golden angel flask and had a quick mug of tea, and a bit of angel cake.

Half an hour later, Maria and John came to Southern Cemetery to lay flowers on Jack's grave. But when they reached the tomb, they saw the stone had been rolled away. John looked into the tomb and saw it was empty. Maria began to cry.

'What have they done to my son now?' she wept.

Then she heard a voice behind her.

'Maria. He is not here. He is risen from the dead.'

She turned round and saw the glowing figure of Eric sitting on the large stone.

'Sir, if you know where he is, please tell me!' she cried.

'He is alive and well. He is risen from the dead! Go and gather the trainees together. Wait in the city and he will come to you.' John and Maria were unsure what Eric meant but clearly something was happening. They ran back to meet the others to tell them about the empty tomb.

oOo

Down at Boggart Hole Clough, the boggarts were on their third day of celebrating. Owd Hob's underground castle was still throbbing with boggart music and dancing. The drinks were still flowing freely.

Suddenly, a loud knock on the door of the main hall brought the party to a standstill. Owd Hob scanned the gathered boggarts and other creatures of darkness. They all seemed to be accounted for.

Owd Hob watched with horror as he saw the handle turn and the door swing open. The boggarts shielded their eyes from the blazing light of the uninvited visitor.

'We meet again,' said Jack.

'But ... you are supposed to be dead!' said Owd Hob, cowering in the light of Jack's presence.

'Well I'm back!' said Jack. 'And I have brought some friends.'

Godfrey stepped through the door and began to sing the song of creation. The boggarts squealed and jammed their fingers in their ears.

Angels of light filed into the room and surrounded the boggarts.

'You have no authority here, Jack!' shouted Owd Hob. 'Remember the Cancer Tree!'

'The Cancer Tree is dead!' said Jack.

'What!?' said Owd Hob.

'And I have brought another friend to see you,' said Jack.

Sophia stepped through the door.

'Noooooooo!' screamed Owd Hob.

Sophia breathed out, and as she did, parts of the room burst into flames.

'It's over!' said Jack.

He gave the signal and the angels attacked. Some boggarts fought back. Others fled down the many underground tunnels leading from the castle.

Owd Hob began to shape-shift. He became the black lion and roared at Godfrey and Jack. But his only weapon was fear, and Godfrey and Jack were not afraid of him. He then changed into a white rat and fled down a boggart hole.

Soon the entire underground castle was in flames and Owd Hob's headquarters were reduced to ashes. The fire burned for three days, and the smoke could be seen from as far away as Salford. The boggarts scattered far and wide as their kingdom was destroyed.

32

The Lamb of Godfrey

The peacocks squawked as Godfrey and Jack rode the tandem up the drive at Brookdale Park. Philip the angel waved to them as he mowed the vast lawns in the restored grounds.

'Wow! The restoration job on this place is amazing!' said Jack, looking towards the white mansion in the grounds of Brookdale.

'All down to Philip and his team of angel helpers,' said Godfrey.

They pulled up at the front entrance to the house and Jack surveyed the freshly painted building.

'This house is better than the previous house!' said Jack.

'It is wonderful, isn't it?' said Godfrey, taking in the view.

'Right! Well, we best get into the kitchen and get to work!' said Jack.

'Hey, Lad,' said Godfrey. 'I think you are about due some time off. After thirty-three years living as a human, and then the events of this last week, I think you should rest a while. I can cook lunch today.'

'I'll not argue with that, Dad. Are you going to do one of your stunning Sunday Roasts?'

'That I am, Jack. Roast lamb and all the trimmings, with sherry trifle for afters.'

'Lush!' said Jack.

Wandering into the library, Jack found new furniture and new books to occupy himself with. As the sunbeams streamed through the windows, Jack could hear Godfrey whistling and banging pans about in the kitchen. He scanned the shelves of the library. He noticed that the angels had restored many of his favourite books but had also provided some new titles.

He found a book he hadn't read before – *"Miracles for Dummies, a guide for the rest of us"*. He sat down in one of the new armchairs. The chair felt so comfortable. Jack began to read, but soon felt drowsy. He closed his eyes to rest them for a moment and was soon gently snoring in the chair.

oOo

Pete, Jim, and the other trainees were all camped out in Bluebell Woods, hiding for fear of the temple managers and the Italian Police. The only ones missing were Ian, who had betrayed Jack, and John, who was looking after Maria.

They were keeping a low profile and unsure what their next move would be. They were still devastated about Jack. As they talked quietly about what they might do, they heard voices in the distance. They hid themselves in the bushes and waited.

To their great relief it was only John and Maria, the

only ones who knew where they were hiding.

John and Maria told the others about the empty tomb and the angel.

'Are you sure you went to the right tomb?' asked Pete.

'You saw a real angel?' asked Jim.

'Yes! Yes! It's all true! He is alive!' said Maria.

'The angel said to wait and Jack would find us,' said John.

'So we just have to wait here?' asked Pete.

'I think so,' said John.

'You saw a real angel?' asked Jim again.

'I'm telling you,' said Maria. 'He is alive!'

As they were speaking, a sudden breeze blew through the camp. It was a warm refreshing sort of breeze. It blew the leaves along the forest floor in a certain direction.

They thought they heard a gentle whisper. They looked at each other. The hair on the back of their necks stood up.

There, a little beyond where they were standing, seemed to be a bright light. They each felt compelled to find out what it was.

Creeping through the woods towards the light, they heard another whisper.

'Come to me all you weary ones, and I will give you rest,' said the voice. It sounded familiar.

Near the light they saw a narrow gate with the words "Welcome. Come in" painted on it.

'Do you think it's him?' whispered Pete.

'Who else could it be?' asked John.

The little group entered through the narrow gate.

oOo

'Wake up sleepy head!' said Godfrey, nudging Jack out of his slumber in the chair. 'Food is just about ready and Sophia says our visitors should arrive any moment now.'

'Huh?' said Jack waking up. 'Oh, right. Yes. Well, we better go and greet them.'

Godfrey and Jack went outside to join Sophia, who was looking down the drive to the narrow gate.

When the little group were still far off, Godfrey ran down the drive to meet them and bring them home.

The trainees were nervously looking round at the amazing grounds, when they saw Godfrey running towards them. They were unsure if they were in trouble, or trespassing.

'Welcome! Welcome! My dear friends!' Godfrey embraced each one and welcomed them by name, then led them up to the house.

'I am so glad you came,' said Godfrey.

'I think you know this young man,' he continued, motioning towards Jack.

The group were open mouthed. They thought they were seeing a ghost.

'Good to see you all again,' said Jack. He embraced Maria, who was so overwhelmed she fainted. Jack caught her and laid her down on a garden bench. He brushed her hair out of her face.

'She'll be fine. She just needs a moment,' said Jack.

As Maria rested on the bench, Jack embraced all the trainees, who were all feeling a bit weak at the knees.

Godfrey introduced them to Sophia and then waved his arms towards Philip and the gardening angels out on the big field. Philip gathered his little band of gardeners and led them up to the house.

'Where am I?' said Maria, coming round. Jack perched on the edge of the bench and stroked his mother's face.

'Have I died and gone to heaven?' asked Maria.

'You haven't died, Mum. You've just come home for a little while.'

Godfrey called everyone to the long table in the main dining hall. Jack brought in all the food Godfrey had cooked, including a roast lamb, and laid it out on the table. 'Behold the lamb!' said Godfrey. 'We have taken away the curse of the world! And now we must celebrate.

Jack took a bread roll from the basket on the table.

'This is my body given for you,' he said, as he tore the bread into pieces. And now they all understood what he had told them in the upstairs room, on the night he was arrested.

'This is my blood of the new arrangement, poured out for you,' said Jack, pouring everyone a glass of red wine. It all seemed obvious now.

Everyone agreed it was the most amazing meal they had ever tasted. And as the little group sat and ate with angels and archangels, and with all the company of heaven, Godfrey told them the story of Manchester and how it had been created. Beginning with Albert and Edna, he explained why all these things had happened, especially the destruction of the Cancer Tree.

John was making lots of notes, as he was still planning to write a book about the life of Jack.

'Is Owd Hob dead then?' asked Pete.

'No. Not yet. But his power is greatly reduced,' said Godfrey. 'He was stripped of his magic powers. The curse he put on humans - making it very difficult to hear or see us - is broken. Now when we call, humans will hear us clearly. They may not all come. Some will still seek out boggarts and darkness. But many will come. And when a human responds to our call, Jack and I will come to them, and make our home with them.'

Jack served up the trifle and everyone loved it.

'Trifle is three distinct things, yet it is one dessert. Three in one. It is a profound thing,' said Jack, as he served it up.

'Now you have found the narrow gate you can come in and out and find refreshment here anytime. In fact, you don't even have to come here. Just call on us wherever you are, and we'll be there!'

Godfrey topped up everyone's drink and led them to the library, where a nice log fire was flickering in the hearth. Godfrey told them a story.

As the food, drink and log fire took effect, the trainees fell asleep in their very comfy chairs. When they awoke, they were in their camp in Bluebell Woods. Either they had all had the same dream, or that afternoon really had happened.

'Didn't our hearts burn with excitement as Godfrey explained the story of Manchester?' said Pete.

'Does anyone else remember Jack telling us to get together in the city centre in fifty days' time?' said Jim.

'Aye, he did say that,' said John.

The trainees laid low for a while as all sorts of rumours were going around about what had happened to Jack's body. The Emperor Julius was unsettled by its disappearance. He assumed the trainees had stolen it so they could start some story about Jack still being alive.

33

Hurricane Sophia

Jack was cooking a full English breakfast at Brookdale. Godfrey and Sophia were having a mug of coffee outside, enjoying the mild air.

'Well it's a lovely day for a visitation,' said Godfrey.

Sophia smiled and sipped her coffee.

Philip and Eric were harvesting fruit in the orchard. It was a big harvest that year.

'So you have found a way to restore the image of Jack into the human soul?' asked Godfrey.

'Yes,' said Sophia. 'The only thing ever stopping me from becoming one with a human was the effect of the Cancer Tree. Now the Cancer Tree has been destroyed by Jack, I can live in any human who welcomes me.'

'Wonderful!' said Godfrey. 'The world will be a different place after today.'

'Don't get your hopes too high,' said Sophia. 'The humans do tend to be a bit self-centred. My living in them will be a gradual change, not the flick of a switch. They will judge and condemn each other often. I can only influence them, not control them. They will retain their own will.'

'Well, yes, that is true,' said Godfrey. 'I am a gardener not an engineer. I never set out to build robots. I was just looking to create creatures who could join our little community. I really wanted friends. I created this whole planet so there could be loving, gracious communities. I didn't really anticipate the rebellion of the boggarts, or their deep, destructive cruelty.'

'Yes, you are a gardener,' said Sophia. 'And when you plant a living thing, it is very hard to know how it will grow. But the nurture and care you have invested in your creation will now produce centuries of good fruit. Quite how it will grow, who knows? Like any garden there will be winters when all looks lost, but then there will be springs and new growth, summers of abundance, and autumns of rest.'

Sophia's reflections were interrupted by Jack.

'It's on the table! Going cold!'

Godfrey smiled.

'He means he is about to serve up,' said Godfrey.

They walked back to the house hand in hand. When they got inside, Godfrey embraced Sophia for a moment.

'You are beautiful,' said Godfrey.

'You're not so bad yourself, for an old gardener,' said Sophia.

Jack was serving up bacon, eggs, beans, sausages, mushrooms and fried bread, followed by toast and marmalade, coffee and croissants.

'What a feast!' said Godfrey.

The three of them ate breakfast and reminisced about the long journey to this special day.

After breakfast, Jack and Godfrey cleared the table and did the washing up. When they came back to the dining room, Sophia was gone.

They went outside and looked down the drive.

'Where did she go?' asked Jack.

'The wind blows where it will,' said Godfrey. 'You cannot see where it comes from or where it goes. But when the wind blows, you will feel the breeze on your face.'

'Well I hope the people of Manchester have battened down the hatches,' said Jack, 'because that is one serious hurricane coming at them!'

'They have no idea what is about to hit them,' said Godfrey.

oOo

Fifty days after Jack rose from the dead, Manchester was busy with visitors for the Festival of Pianocost – the time of year when the people remembered when Godfrey gave Martin Simmonite the special piano, with the ten tips for a good life.

Many people had travelled into Manchester for the festival and the city was buzzing.

The trainees had all gathered together just as Jack had told them to do. They were meeting in the tea room just off Piccadilly. They had just finished breakfast when suddenly the wind began to blow outside. The wind got stronger and stronger. Things began to blow down the street outside. Then the door of the tea room blew open and the gale force wind blew through the shop. Chairs blew over.

The trainees didn't know what to do. Then, right in the middle of the tea room they saw a glowing figure.

They recognised Sophia. She seemed to be surrounded by flames. Dazzling light filled the whole place. Then the flames seemed to spread to the trainees as each one of them began to glow; the life force of Sophia was being poured into them. They began to laugh. Some cried with joy. The experience was so wonderful they didn't know if they could contain it.

They staggered out of the tea room and into Piccadilly Gardens, still laughing. The wind was still blowing hard. All the people wondered what was happening. The trainees began to speak in different dialects.

A crowd had gathered and were confused. 'Are they not all Mancunian, who speak?' One of them shouted. 'How is it that we hear each in our own dialect - Scousers, Geordies, Brummies, Scots, Irish, Welsh - the wonderful works of Godfrey? What does this mean?'

Others mocked the trainees, saying they were just a bunch of drunks.

Then Pete stood up, raised his voice and addressed them. 'Men of Britain and Ireland, let this be known to you. We are not drunk, as you say. It's only nine o'clock in the morning!'

He told the people about the day at Jack's mansion when they had all seen him alive and well, and that what they were seeing, right now, was the life force of Godfrey being breathed into human hearts. Many of the people were deeply moved and asked what they should do.

'Become thoughtful,' said Pete, 'and turn, in your heart, to Godfrey. Call to him and he will come to you. He will change your life and take the deep sadness from your hearts. He will repay you for the years the locusts have eaten.'

As Pete spoke, he noticed that some of Sophia's flames were spreading from him to the people. It was as though the life force of Godfrey was being poured out on every human.

34

Afterwards

What happened after that day is well documented in other books. The trainee, John, did write his book about Jack's life as a human. He also published three letters to some new trainees, which make interesting reading. John also wrote a sequel when he was arrested by the Italians and put in jail, but it was a bit deep and few people understood it. The local GP, Dr Luke, also wrote about those times and what happened after. Pete told the story to a young lad called Mark, who rushed to publish first, while Matthew, a tax inspector, also wrote a book about Jack. They are all worth reading.

But what really happened after all of this?

Well, after centuries of Mancunians longing to overthrow the brutal Italian occupation, they didn't have to worry in the end. So many Italian leaders were connecting to the boggart kingdom that the Italian Empire simply collapsed under the weight of its own corruption. Italian forces were withdrawn from Manchester, as they had more important wars at home in Italy.

Manchester was restored to the Mancunians, who rebuilt many parts of their great city.

As for Godfrey, Jack and Sophia, well, they are still very much around, but they wait for humans to call on them. But here and there, now and then, if you walk on the Mountains of Ninepence – or the Pennines as they are called today – you can sometimes hear Godfrey laughing or singing in the wind. Or you may hear Jack calling to you, or feel a gentle breeze from Sophia, though you won't see them.

Godfrey's Tower still stands at Hartshead Pike but he's moved to a new place now. He prefers to live in the hearts of humans. Each one of us can be Godfrey's tower, if we allow him to live in our hearts.

About the author

Don Egan grew up in Manchester. His early summers were spent in Brookdale Park in Newton Heath. He has walked and cycled to Hartshead Pike many times. Don attended All Saints Primary School, in Newton Heath and then North Manchester High School for boys, in Blackley. He worked in factories in Chadderton and Ancoats, and then in social work in Moss Side before training for ministry in the Church of England.

He has addressed thousands of people in Africa, Asia and Europe.

He now lives in Suffolk where he leads RSVP Trust – a charity that transforms lives in the UK and Africa.

For more information about Don Egan, or to book him for speaking engagements, please visit:

www.rsvptrust.co.uk

Connect

Twitter
@Don_Egan
Facebook
www.facebook.com/chroniclesofgodfrey
www.facebook.com/rsvpdonegan